It was eleven o'clock ... clock and knew that ...ming. She turned away, her mo... ...to a false smile, but inwardly she was cursing herself for a fool; she had never *really* believed that her mother would come, even though she'd promised several times over. But there had always been a small, lingering hope that the engagement party of her only child would be a sufficiently special enough occasion for the famous Adele Verlaine to put in an appearance. But earlier that evening Michelle had received a telephone message from her mother's secretary saying that the rehearsal for her new play was running late and she would try to get down later.

But of course she hadn't arrived. She never did. Michelle had received the same type of excuse dozens of times before: at school parents' days, when she was waiting to be taken on a promised outing, and often even on the day before long looked-forward-to holidays. All cancelled at a moment's notice, leaving her as a child bewildered and weeping, and as a teenager with tight, set face and a hurt that showed only in her eyes. Even now, at nineteen, when she should have been used to it, the hurt was still there, hidden behind the bright smile; that, and increasing humiliation.

'My dance, I think, m'dear.'

Mr Milner, Peter's father, came to put a proprietorial hand under her elbow and led her on to the dance floor. Michelle smiled at him and tried to look as if she meant it as he took her round in a rather ponderous waltz.

'Doesn't look as if your mother's going to be able to make it after all,' he remarked with real disappointment in his voice. 'Damn shame,' he went on. 'But then she's so dedicated, such a professional actress. Not many women would be prepared to forgo their daughter's engagement party for the sake of their art.'

'No,' Michelle agreed drily. 'Very few, I imagine.'

But he wasn't listening. 'Remarkable woman, your mother. Never met anyone quite like her. Definitely the most charming woman I've ever met.'

Oh, yes, she was charming all right, Michelle thought bitterly as he went rabbiting on. Her mother's beauty, warmth and vitality had a stunning effect which won people over and made them her ardent fans for life. A talent which had captured and held theatre audiences the world over and helped to make her one of the most famous and sought-after actresses of the decade. The charm, too, carried over into Adele Verlaine's private life; Michelle could remember time and time again falling under its spell as her mother effusively apologised for a broken promise, showered her with expensive toys and made lots more solemn promises which she never kept. And even now nothing had changed; she still used gifts as a substitute for love. Michelle looked sourly at the diamond bracelet on her wrist, a companion to the pendant round her neck and the pair of stud earrings given to her the day before by her mother's secretary with a verbal message. She hadn't even found the time to send a note with them. No, Michelle was one of the two people in the world on whom her mother's 'charm' had worn very thin.

'Have you decided on a date for the wedding yet?'

Michelle tried to give Mr Milner her attention—after all, it wasn't his fault that her mother had let her down on one of the most important days in her life, and he and his wife had really been very kind, taking over this Thameside night club for the evening and inviting so many of her friends as well as all Peter's friends and family.

'Not yet,' she answered. 'Though we did think perhaps September, in about four months' time.'

'Splendid,' he enthused. 'Not too long for you young people to have to wait but still giving plenty of time to make all the arrangements.' He hesitated for a moment and cleared his throat. 'I wonder, perhaps you might have a word with Adele —with your mother—and ask her if she'd like to leave all the wedding arrangements to us? I know how busy she is, you see. She told me so when she very kindly sent us the tickets for her last play and invited us backstage to meet her. All she need do really is to get together with us once or twice, over lunch or dinner perhaps, and let us know what she wants done, give us her list of guests, that kind of thing. It would be a pleasure to save her all that boring work.'

Well, that at least was true, Michelle thought with increased bitterness; she would certainly find arranging her daughter's wedding a bore.

But Mr Milner's voice was growing animated as he went on, 'I expect there are a great many of her friends, actors and playwrights, that she'll want to invite. And then there's your father—he's in America, isn't he?'

'Yes, he lives there permanently now.'

'You'll have to give me his address so that I can write to him. He's bound to want to know that you're marrying into a respectable family and what Peter's prospects are. And we must offer to put him up when he comes over for the wedding.'

Michelle made some non-committal reply, not at all certain that her father, whom she hadn't seen for several years, would want to come to her wedding.

When the dance ended Peter came to claim her and introduced her to a couple of his old school friends who had been in the rugger team with him. They were interrupted after only a few minutes, though, by a waiter bringing round a tray of champagne, and the music stopped as Peter's father made a speech welcoming her to their family and then proposed a toast to the betrothed couple. Michelle smiled dutifully as everyone drank to them, but would have been better pleased if Mr Milner hadn't mentioned her mother's name three times and her father's twice.

Then it was Peter's turn to make an answering speech, which he did after some shouts of encouragement from the guests and one or two modest refusals on his part. He took her hand in his while he spoke, her left one with the brilliant new engagement ring on the third finger. He began by saying, 'Oh, dear, this is a complete surprise,' then went on to make a very good 'impromptu' speech; but Michelle had lived among actors all her life and knew a prepared piece when she heard it. She watched him as he spoke; quite fair, quite tall, quite handsome, and proud as Punch with himself. Well, he had reason to be, didn't he? Michelle told herself roundly. At twenty-two he already had a middling university degree behind him and could look forward to a safe career as first an assistant and then a partner in his father's stockbroking firm in the City. Everything had always gone well for him all his life without too much effort on his part; just brainy enough to get into university, just good enough to get into the first rugger team, and just handsome enough to get engaged to Michelle Bryant, the only child of the brilliant theatrical couple Adele Verlaine and Sir Richard Bryant. No matter that the famous husband and wife team had split up and been divorced years ago, they still acted together often enough for their names to be linked in the minds of theatre and cinemagoers the world over.

There was another burst of applause after Peter's speech and then someone handed her a glass of champagne so that they could drink to each other. He smiled warmly down at her as he did so and Michelle tried to make her smile in return just as warm, but somehow it didn't quite come off. But Peter didn't notice because all the younger guests were calling for him to kiss her. He laughed, bending her back to kiss her on the mouth, harder and far longer than was necessary, so that his friends gave whoops of encouragement and the rest of her champagne spilt on the floor. At last he let her go, flushed and laughing.

Michelle's face, too, was flushed, from embarrassment. She knew that it had been just bravado in front of his friends, but she didn't appreciate Peter's using her like that in public. Quickly she moved away from him and held out her empty glass for a waiter to refill and rather defiantly drank it down in a couple of swallows. The rest of the evening settled down into dances with men she'd just met that night, chats with their wives and daughters, polite smiles and laughter, constantly hearing Peter's parents dropping her mother's or her father's name, and enough glasses of champagne so that she didn't much care anyway.

'When was it your father received his knighthood,

my dear?' Mr Milner asked her. 'Just after his brilliant performance in *Othello* at Stratford, wasn't it?
Yes, I'm sure it was.' He turned back to the people
he was speaking to without waiting for her to answer
and went on with his monologue on her father's
career.

Michelle groaned inwardly; it was just pure bad
luck that Peter's people should have turned out to
be such ardent theatre-lovers. They had been over
the moon at the news of the engagement and had
really caught the celebrity bug since they'd been
introduced to her mother. That they had only met
on the one occasion and Adele Verlaine, recognising
the symptoms, had kept them at the end of a long
telephone line ever since, didn't seem to make any
difference at all; they still brought her parents' names
into the conversation whenever possible. As she stood
there listening, it gradually dawned on Michelle that
this party hadn't been arranged for Peter's and her
own pleasure at all, but merely in the hope that her
mother would put in an appearance and perhaps
bring some of her famous friends with her, possibly
even Patrick O'Keefe, the volatile Irish actor that
rumour had it she was contemplating marrying. Not
that she ever would; sharing the limelight once had
been enough to peel off most of Adele Verlaine's
layers of charm so that her husband had seen
through her; she would never make that mistake
again, Michelle knew.

Feeling an arm go round her waist, Michelle
turned and saw Peter by her side.

'Come and dance,' he said possessively.

Obediently she finished off the glass of wine she
was holding and let him take it from her and lead
her on to the dance floor. He pulled her close against
him and she stumbled a little, then giggled as she

put her hand on his shoulder to support herself. Peter laughed and pulled her closer. His face was still flushed and she could smell whisky on his breath.

'All my friends keep asking me when we're going to get married,' he said in her ear. 'But I told them that's only a formality. God, who waits till their wedding nowadays?'

'Oh, Peter, really! You don't have to tell everyone, do you?'

He laughed again and kissed her clumsily on the cheek. 'There's nothing to tell yet, is there?'

The band changed to a fast beat number, coloured psychedelic lights threw patterns on the ceiling and walls of the darkened room and most of the guests, old and young alike, crowded on to the floor to let their hair down in their own way. Michelle swayed and gyrated in the crush until Peter caught her arm and pulled her towards the edge.

'Come on, let's get out of here.'

Picking up a full bottle of champagne and a couple of glasses from a nearby table, he propelled her towards some French doors leading on to a lawn which sloped down towards the river. There were already one or two couples standing in the shadows, locked in close embrace, but Peter pulled her round the angle of the building and towards the car park at the side.

'Wait! Where are we going?' Michelle found it difficult to keep up with him in the long tight dress she was wearing.

'To my car. Come on.'

She stopped and tried to pull away. 'Peter, we can't! People will notice we've gone.'

'No, they won't—they're all too busy dancing. And anyway, what does it matter if they do?'

'Because it's supposed to be our party, that's why.

No, Peter, they're bound to notice.'

He moved towards her and put his free arm round her waist. 'Just five minutes, then. Come on, darling. We haven't had any time alone together all evening. I haven't even had a chance to tell you properly how lovely you look.'

'Oh, all right.' Michelle let him lead her along. 'But only for five minutes, mind.'

'Of course.'

They reached his blue hatchback that had been a twenty-first birthday present from his parents, and he quickly took the keys from his pocket and opened the door. Once inside, he immediately opened the bottle of champagne, and they both laughed as the cork banged against the roof and the liquid frothed out and splashed them.

'Here's to us,' Peter toasted. 'Come on, drink it all down in one go.'

Gigglingly Michelle did as she was told, and as soon as her glass was empty Peter took it from her and put it on the floor, then took her in his arms and began to kiss her possessively, his hands hot and clumsy as they fumbled with the straps of her dress. He pulled them down and then his hands were on her breasts, stroking, exploring. Michelle returned his kiss, letting him do what he wanted until he squeezed too hard and hurt her.

'No!' She pushed him away. 'Peter, you said just five minutes!'

'We've hardly been here two yet. Come on, let's have another drink.'

They drank more champagne and he got her laughing before he started to make love to her again. Michelle's head felt strangely as if it was a long way above her neck, and this time she didn't fight him off until he'd lifted her skirt and tried to put his hand up it. Peter sat back, his breathing heavy and his hands shaking. He poured himself another glass of wine and drank it down in one gulp, then insisted she do the same.

'No, I don't want any more.'

'Yes, you do. You've had hardly any yet. And we might as well finish the bottle.'

By bullying and persuasion he got her to drink another two glasses and by then Michelle could hardly even see straight.

'Michelle—oh, darling, you're so sweet. I love you, darling.' His hands seemed to be everywhere, and she gasped as he let down the back of her seat and rolled on top of her.

'No, Peter. No!' She tried to protest as he pulled her skirt up round her waist, but her voice wouldn't come out the way she wanted it to and her hands seemed to have no strength in them when she tried to push him away. His hand pulled at her underclothes and she moaned as he touched her. For a while sexuality took over and she stopped fighting, but then she gave a violent, explosive, 'No!' as she jerked up into a sitting position and pushed him violently away.

'Get away from me, or I'll scream the place down!' she yelled at him, real fright and panic in her voice.

'Come on, you know you want to,' Peter persisted, trying to kiss her again.

'No, I don't! You keep away from me!'

'Aw, for heaven's sake, Michelle!' Peter sat up and raised a trembling hand to push his hair out of his eyes. His voice was slurred and unsteady, his forehead wet with beads of perspiration. 'You promised we could do it when we got engaged.'

'But I didn't mean in the middle of our engagement party,' Michelle told him angrily. 'And I sure as hell didn't mean on the front seat of a car either!'

'Well, if that's all you're worried about we can go down to the river. There are some bushes there and we won't be seen by . . .'

'No!' Michelle said furiously. 'Can't you understand? I don't want to.'

'Yes, you do. You know you do really.' He started to kiss her again, forcing her head back, and his hand groped for her breast.

'Leave me alone!' She tried to push him away, but he was stronger than she was and she couldn't move him.

'Please, Michelle, please.' His breath was hot and alcoholic near her face, his hands once again trying to pull up her skirt. 'I want you so much, darling. And I love you, I really do. Don't you love me?'

'Oh, Peter, you know I do.'

'Well then, prove it to me.'

'No. Not here, not like this.'

'Just this once. We'll do it properly in a bed next time, I promise.'

'No! Haven't you any feelings?'

But he refused to listen, using all his strength to push her down again, clawing at her clothes. With a sob of anger and fear, Michelle realised that she couldn't fight him off no matter how much she hit out at him and tried to push him away. Tears began to run down her cheeks when he wouldn't listen to her protests, and her head felt so strange, as if it didn't belong to her any more. Feebly she tried to push him away again, and for a moment thought that she had been successful as he drew back, but then she realised that he was fumbling with his trousers, pulling them down.

Panic-stricken, Michelle groped for the door handle, found it, and almost fell out of the car, losing one of her shoes in the process.

'Michelle! Don't! What the hell are you doing?' Peter made a grab for her and caught her dress, tried to pull her back.

With a tremendous effort that sent her reeling, she managed to pick herself up and pull away, the material of her dress tearing in the desperate tug-of-war. Still sobbing with fear, she ran out of the car park, down towards the darkness of the river bank. Her one high-heeled shoe impeded her and she had to stop to take it off, her heart beating crazily in case Peter caught her. But then the shoe was off and she was running down through the soft grass, away from the glare of the night club's lights towards the blessed darkness where she could hide among the bushes.

She'd hardly reached them and cowered down among their foliage before she heard Peter calling her name. He was still some distance away, near the car park, she judged, and wondered why it had taken him so long to come after her. Then she felt an insane impulse to giggle hysterically as she realised that he'd literally been caught with his pants down. Hastily she stuffed a hand into her mouth, but laughter soon gave way to fear again when she remembered that Peter had suggested they go to these very bushes to make love. This was the first place he would come and look for her and he would be bound to see her in her white dress. And if he found her here she wouldn't be able to stop him—and the dress wouldn't be virginal white any longer.

Desperately Michelle tried to look round into the darkness for somewhere else to hide. There were some lights from boats on the river, but her head was swimming so much that they somehow got mixed up with the stars. The tide must be quite high, she could hear the water lapping gently against the river bank and she had the wild idea of trying to find a boat and rowing to the other side. Crawling nearer to the water's edge under cover of the trailing bushes, she groped hopefully for a rope, or some other sign of a boat; if there was one on the bank she might be able to hide underneath it. Her mind an incoherent jumble of hopes and fears, she stumbled along, and gave an involuntary cry of pain as a thorn tore at her arm.

'Michelle? Michelle, is that you?'

Peter's voice, much closer than she had expected, made her jump with alarm and she turned round to run in the opposite direction, farther down the river bank. Clumsily she pushed the bushes aside, wincing with pain as the thorns caught at her, making her drop her shoe as she put up her hands to protect her face. Her breath came in little sobbing pants as she stumbled on, then turned to a gasp of fear as she heard Peter pushing through the bushes behind her. She looked quickly round to see if she could see him, but the quick movement sent her brain into dizzying spirals as she swayed drunkenly and the stars went whizzing in circles round her head. She teetered, half falling, and reeled backwards, putting out her arms to try to steady herself, but suddenly there was nothing under her feet any more and she fell ungracefully backwards into the river.

Her cry of surprise rather than fear, and the splash she made, brought an answering shout from Peter. 'Michelle? Where are you?'

Spluttering and gasping, she came to the surface and made a grab for a root that was sticking out of the muddy bank.

'P-Peter! Help!' The water was cold, so cold. And the current was strong, she could feel it tugging at her legs, already weighted down by the sopping material of her dress and slip.

'Michelle?' The white blob of Peter's face appeared above her. 'You stupid idiot! Why did you run away from me? Here, take my hand and I'll pull you out.'

He reached down towards her, but the bank was steep here and, although Michelle stretched her arm up as far as she could, there was still at least a foot gap between them.

'Come on.' Impatiently Peter eased himself a little further forward. 'Try and pull yourself up by that root you're holding on to.'

'I am trying. But it's slippery, and my skirt's heavy. Oh, God, it's so cold!' Using both hands, she pulled on the root and tried to bring her feet on to the bank to lever herself upwards, but then the fibrous root bulged out towards her, there was a tearing sound and it broke away from the bank in a shower of mud and stones as she was carried, still clinging to it, downstream with the tide.

Her first reaction was to scream, but as she did so Michelle fell back into the river and her open mouth filled with rank, oily water. Fighting her way to the surface, she came up coughing and spitting out the foul-tasting liquid. Vaguely behind her she could hear Peter shouting her name, but it was too dark to see where she was and she could hardly make out the darker mass of the bank. She tried to kick out towards it, but the current was much too strong and she was carried fast along with it, clinging to the root as if her life depended upon it, but her head going under more and more often as her struggles to stay afloat gradually weakened.

Half drowned as she was, it wasn't until it rubbed against her arm that Michelle realised the root had got entangled with a rope. Quickly she let go the root and caught hold of the wet nylon rope, using all her remaining strength to pull herself up out of the water a little and gasp some air into her lungs. But the tide was still strong, still pulling at her legs and trying to draw her back into its power. Dimly she could see the outline of a boat above her with the soft green glow of a light farther down the deck. Weakly she called for help, but the occupants mustn't have heard her, because no one came. Her arms began to burn in their sockets as the current tried to pluck her away and she shouted again, her voice hysterical with fear. Then, for a brief moment, the moon came out and she saw a swimming platform and short ladder at the back of the boat that reached down into the water. If she could only reach it! It was only a yard or so away, but to get there she would have to let go of the rope and swim at an angle against the current. And once she'd let go of the rope, if she missed the back of the boat ... Michelle shuddered and called for help again, her voice rising to a scream, but still no one came. Her hands slid a few inches down the wet rope and she realised sickeningly that if she didn't try now her strength would all be gone and she wouldn't stand any chance of making it. With a great sob, she forced herself to let go of the rope and kicked out towards the ladder.

Her left hand caught one of the rungs, slipped off and she was carried past, but then her right hand clutched at the corner of the boat and somehow she managed to pull herself back and get a firm grip on the metal side of the ladder. She had to rest then, panting for breath before she could manage to climb up the ladder and pull herself over the rail.

The green and red riding lights cast an eerie glow over the shadowed deck, but at least they gave her enough light to see the door leading down to the cabins. Shaking with cold, her teeth chattering, Michelle banged on the door and called out, but there was no reply and she realised at last that the boat must be empty. Without hope, she pushed at the cabin door and stood stock-still in amazement when it swung open. Quickly then she went inside, groped for a light switch and turned it on. She found herself in a large saloon but had to turn and go down some more steps to a lower deck before she found a galley and beyond it the sleeping cabins. Michelle didn't know much about boats, but she was pretty sure that there ought to be some sort of bathroom where she might find a towel to rub herself dry.

After the galley there were double cabins on either side, but then she found a bathroom and gratefully stripped off the soggy remnants of her dress, her torn tights and her bra and pants, letting them lie in a heap on the floor as she wrapped a big soft towel round herself and began to rub some life into her numb limbs. The towel caught on her necklace and it took several minutes to remove that and her bracelet and earrings, and of course her engagement ring. Michelle looked at it resentfully, wishing she'd thought to throw it back at Peter. The beast! She hoped he was still looking for her and going mad with worry.

Dropping the jewels on to a shelf above the hand basin, she glanced up and caught sight of herself in the mirror. God, she looked terrible! Her long brown hair hung in a tangled mass about her shoulders, and her hazel eyes were red-rimmed from the river. Her mascara had run and made black patches under her eyes and there was a scratch down the side of her cheek from a thorn or something. Michelle gazed at herself miserably, hating her face. She'd always hated it, a cross between her parents' features that had little of her mother's exceptional beauty and none of her father's strength of character, only his leanness and high cheekbones. Even now, when she felt half dead, when only all the alcohol she'd drunk prevented her from fainting from cold, she could still look at her reflection disparagingly. Echoes of her mother's, 'But you have quite a pleasant face, darling', and her father's, 'Never mind, little one, you can always play character parts', rang in her ears from long, long ago.

Suddenly the room began to sway and she had to cling to the sink; nausea filled her throat, but she managed to fight it down. Lord, she was so cold, and so tired! Through the muzziness in her head, she realised that she couldn't stay here, she would have to try and find someone to help her, get her some dry clothes. Still wrapped in the towel, she reeled unsteadily along, exploring the rest of the boat and finding that only one of the cabins seemed to be occupied, a single one in the forward end. This had the bunk made up with a soft comfortable-looking sleeping bag and there were some books on a shelf, and a man's clothes in the wardrobe. Michelle looked at both the clothes and the sleeping bag longingly, wondering what to do. But her head felt so heavy that she could hardly keep her eyes open and took the choice away from her. Fumblingly she found the zip of the sleeping bag and pulled it down, then dropped the towel and climbed in just as she was, snuggling down into its soft enfolding warmth. Within two minutes she had fallen into a deep, drunken sleep.

Her first sensation on waking was to an agonising pain in her head. She groaned and found that her throat and lips felt terribly dry, and there was a queer, unpleasant sensation in her stomach. She moaned again and tried to sit up, blinking in the bright glare of the bedside light. Sitting up was a mistake; it sent sharp pains up into her head and made her stomach feel more queasy than ever. Closing her eyes against the glare, Michelle leant back and felt the coldness of wood touching her bare shoulders. Not up to opening her eyes and turning her head to look, she tried to work out why she wasn't wearing any pyjamas and why the headboard should feel cold and wooden when she knew quite well that the headboard of her bed in her mother's London flat was soft, padded velvet.

At length the knives being pushed into her brain eased a little and she managed to very tentatively open one eye. Realisation that she wasn't at home in her own bed but on a boat came at once, and she stared round the little cabin in bewilderment. The walls were panelled in varnished wood, there was a rich deep red carpet on the floor and curtains of a toning but lighter shade pulled across the window. Everything looked clean and new, and a faint smell of the fresh varnish still lingered in the air. Slowly, gingerly, Michelle sat up a little bit more and tried to work out where she was and how she'd got there, but her poor head was such a jumbled up mass of pain and fleeting impressions that she soon gave it up.

The glare from the lamp was worse now that she was sitting up, so she groped for the switch and turned it off. The relief to her eyes was immediate, but after a moment or two, when her eyes had adjusted, she saw that the cabin was quite light anyway as daylight filtered through the curtains. Curiosity overcoming her hangover, she reached up and pulled the curtain back, blinking as sunlight poured through the window. Outside there were a whole lot of other boats, some of them large cargo ships, most of which were moored to buoys, but there were several passing through an open stretch of grey sea in-between the massed ships, all guarded by high, massively thick stone harbour walls. Her eyes opened wide in astonishment as she tried to take it all in, and she rubbed them hard, hoping that she was dreaming or something, but when she opened them again all the boats were still there, and now a big ferryboat with the British Rail emblem on its funnel and DOVER–CALAIS painted on the side was surging into the harbour.

'My God! I'm in Dover!' Stupefied, she stared out of the window for several minutes, trying desperately to remember how she'd got here. She could remember going to the engagement party all right, and her mother not turning up, and, very, very vaguely, there was something about being in a car with Peter, but that was as far as it went; trying to search farther through the dentist's drill noises in her head only made it ache worse than ever.

Licking her dry lips, she leant back again and longed for a long, cool drink of water. Her mouth felt absolutely foul. She tried to just forget everything and snuggle down again in the sleeping bag, but physical discomfort at last made her swing her legs off the bunk and stand up. Immediately everything began to sway and she had to put a hand on the wall to steady herself; she hadn't realised that the boat was pitching that much. Her feet became entangled in the towel and she automatically picked it up and wrapped it round her. Tentatively she opened the door and poked her head out. The corridor was deserted, the boat completely quiet. The bathroom was easy to find for the simple reason that she'd left the door open last night. Her discarded clothes were still lying where she'd left them, still soaking wet. Michelle looked at them in shocked horror and slowly the memory of being in the river permeated through to her dulled brain. She shuddered, once again feeling the cold, then shook it off as she searched for a glass. There was only a plastic beaker which she found in a cabinet, but the water tasted absolutely delicious, lubricating her parched throat and taking some of the horrid taste away. Also in the cabinet she found a couple of unopened bars of soap. She looked longingly at them and at the shower. Surely whoever's boat it was wouldn't mind her having a shower. She reached for the soap and then jumped with fright, her hand frozen in mid-air as a voice shouted just outside the window.

For a moment she didn't know what to do, her heart thumping in panic-stricken dismay, then she nearly hit the roof again as another voice shouted almost above her head. She gave a gasping sob as she looked wildly round, but then she realised with a sick feeling of relief that the two voices were outside and had begun to talk to each other; they hadn't been shouting at her at all.

Peering out of the small, round window, she saw that a motorboat with two uniformed men in it had come alongside the boat and had thrown a rope to some unseen person on the deck; the owner of the other voice, presumably. The uniforms puzzled her; she couldn't remember seeing any like that before. But then one of the men stepped up on to the deck of her boat and said, '*Bonjour, m'sieur. Ça va?*' and she leant back against the wall in consternation. Dear God, she wasn't in Dover at all—she was in Calais!

The boat rocked a little as the second uniformed man climbed on board and then the voices faded as

they moved towards the back of the boat. Michelle
stood stock-still, hardly daring to breathe. She
couldn't possibly be in France—could she? It must
take hours and hours for a boat to get from the
Thames to Calais. But this was a big boat, which
probably had quite powerful engines. Belatedly she
looked at her watch, but it had stopped at one-thirty,
presumably the time she'd fallen in the water.
Desperately she tried to force her mind to think, but
all it came up with was that the two uniformed men
were probably French Customs officers, that they
would search the boat and find her. Hastily she
lurched across to the door and pushed home the bolt,
then leaned against it, fearfully waiting for the
moment when someone would come along, find it
locked and demand that she open it.

But, although she strained her ears there was no
sound of searching, she couldn't hear anything at
all. Cautiously she opened the door a fraction,
listened again, then peeped out. The boat was as
quiet as it had been before. She hesitated, wondering
whether to run back to the cabin, wishing she knew
more of what was going on. Then the sound of
someone laughing came faintly to her ears and she
realised that the men were in the galley at the end of
the corridor. If only she could hear what they were
saying she might be able to find out something.
Wrapping the towel tighter round her, Michelle
crept out and tiptoed silently down the carpeted
corridor. The door to the galley was a wooden one,
but it was just a fraction ajar. Putting first her eyes
and then her ear to it, she found that she couldn't
see a thing and could only hear the murmur of
voices, not distinguish the words. Biting her lip, she
put out a tentative finger and by minute fractions of an
inch gradually pushed the door open a little wider.

The voices became clear first and fortunately they were now speaking English. One of the Frenchmen seemed to be asking some technical questions about the boat and a masculine English voice, deep and unhurried, was answering. By squinting at the crack Michelle was able to see the Frenchman, he was sitting at a table and filling in a form, with a glass of what looked like wine at his elbow, but she couldn't see the other Customs man or the owner of the English voice.

'You will be staying long in France, *m'sieur*?' the Frenchman asked.

'No. Just long enough for me to go ashore and pick up some goods waiting for me in the dock. Then I'll be leaving immediately and heading west again.'

'The nature of these goods?'

'Some French wines and cheeses. And also one or two fittings for the boat and some spares. It's all been cleared through Customs and Excise already and is just waiting for me to pick up.'

'You will not be taking anything ashore, *m'sieur* . . .' the man looked at a passport lying on the table, 'M'sieur Farringdon?'

'No, nothing.'

'*Eh bien.*' The man pressed a heavy metal stamp on to an ink pad and stamped the passport, then held it out. 'There is no one else with you, *m'sieur*?'

Michelle's view was suddenly obscured by a broad back in a dark shirt as the boat owner came to take the proffered document. 'No, I'm sailing alone.'

The back moved away and she saw the Frenchman stand up. Quickly she drew away and ran back to the bathroom, trying to remember what she'd heard through her splitting headache. The most important thing, of course, was that the owner of the boat was going straight back to England. And it was also obvious that he had no idea she was aboard. It came to her that if she told him she was here now, after he had told the Frenchman that there was no one else on board, he might not be any too pleased. In fact it might be better all round if he didn't know anything about her being there at all. Michelle stood in the bathroom and tried to think how long it would take to get back to England. From the position of the sun she judged it to be about midday, so there was every hope that they would get back before dark and she could hide in the cabin without being found. The boat moved a little again and she peeped out, to see the two Frenchmen boarding their motorboat. It drew away and then a pair of legs in denim jeans walked along the deck past her window, going towards the back of the boat.

Hastily she dropped down out of sight, although it would have been impossible for anyone to have seen her at that angle. The back of the boat swayed for a moment and then the sound of an outboard motor starting up came from close by and gradually faded away. Michelle let out her breath on a long sigh, realising that the owner must have gone to collect his cargo, which gave her a breathing space in which to decide what to do. Still sitting on the floor, she leant her pounding head against the wall and tried to figure out what to do for the best. The more she thought about staying hidden until they got back to England, the better she liked it; the Englishman's voice had sounded too firm and assured for her liking. She could imagine the ticking off he might give her. No, better to stay hidden until they got back to London and he left the boat. How she was to leave it herself she didn't bother to try to work out; she could always shout to another boat or something. With any luck he wouldn't go to the cabin at all, but it might be better if she moved into one of the main empty ones. But he was bound to go into the bathroom at some time; she was surprised he hadn't used it already and found her clothes there.

Fumblingly she picked up her dress and tried to wring as much water as possible out of it, hoping that it would be dry by the time she got back to England, and shuddering at the thought of having to wear it. Her bra and pants, being nylon, weren't quite so wet, but they were still too damp to put on. She carried the things into one of the main cabins and looked around for somewhere to hang them, finally having to hook them over a wardrobe door. Then she went back for her jewellery and checked that she hadn't left anything else behind. Which left the problem of the towel. Painfully Michelle forced her splitting head to work. Would he miss the towel? She decided that he would and regretfully hung it on the rail. Back in the main cabin she put the jewels safely away in a drawer and then looked round rather helplessly. The bunks just had divans on them, there were no bedclothes or anything she could use to cover herself. She couldn't just stay in here stark naked!

She groaned and forced herself to walk back to the small cabin where she again looked in the wardrobe, but there was nothing apart from a couple of lounge suits, a black evening suit, and several shirts still in their laundry wrappers. Certainly nothing she could use to wear. Damn the man, she thought irritably as she pulled out the drawers of a built-in dresser and slammed them shut again, doesn't he even wear pyjamas? Disconsolately she sat down on the bunk and eyed the sleeping-bag longingly, wondering whether the owner would notice if he came into the cabin and found it gone. But of course he was bound to. She stood up again and the bunk creaked and moved as she did so. It suddenly got through to her aching head that where there was a bunk there might also be a locker. Lifting up the bag and the mattress, Michelle saw that they had been resting on a wooden board which had a hand-wide hole cut into it. Without much hope she lifted the board which hinged easily upwards, and then struck gold! Inside the locker was a spare sleeping-bag, brand new and still in its wrapper. Gleefully she took it out and then tidied the cabin as best she could, not that she could remember how it had looked when she found it, but just hoped the owner wouldn't notice anything amiss.

Back in the cabin she'd chosen, she carefully bolted the door and then spread the sleeping-bag out on the bunk, climbing into it gratefully, her head now so bad that all she wanted to do was lie down and close her eyes. But even as she climbed on to the bunk the sound of an outboard engine came surging nearer to the boat, and she cautiously lifted up the edge of the drawn curtain and looked out. The boat owner was coming back with his cargo. He came up to the back of the boat, skilfully turned the dinghy so that he was broadside on, caught the ladder and cut the engine of the outboard motor at the same time. For a few moments he was out of sight, but then he stood up to unload the cargo and Michelle saw his face for the first time. He was younger than she'd expected, about thirty or so, she guessed, and he had dark hair blown into disarray by the breeze. But she had been right about the firmness, though; there was a hard, tough look to the set of his jaw, the thin line of his mouth, and his cool grey eyes. It was the sort of face that would give short shrift to anyone who annoyed him or he thought a fool.

Michelle shivered and quickly dropped the curtain back in place, hoping against hope that he wouldn't try the cabin door. For a while she lay fearfully listening to his movements along the deck as he stowed the cargo, but at length the pain in her head overcame her anxiety and she closed her eyes and fell asleep.

A ghastly, rolling sensation in her stomach brought her awake fast. She gave a coughing, choking gasp that immediately brought a vile, nauseous feeling into her throat. Putting a hand up to her mouth and trying desperately not to be sick, she almost fell out of the bunk and groped for the door, hardly realising that the cabin was now in darkness. Somehow she managed to fumble open the bolt and reel across the passageway to the bathroom before she lost control and was horribly sick into the loo. She knelt there, retching painfully for some time, only then aware that the boat was pitching and rolling quite badly. With a moan of sheer misery, she pulled herself upright, washed out her mouth, and remembered to flush the loo before staggering back to the cabin and collapsing into the sleeping-bag, heartily wishing she was dead. She lay there in a huddled ball, groaning wretchedly and not thinking about anything except her stomach and her head, and praying for it soon to be over.

Suddenly the light was switched on and she dimly realised that someone had come in and was towering over her. A man exclaimed, 'Good God!' in a stunned tone and she recognised the voice of the boat owner, but she was too ill to have cared less.

Hopefully she opened her eyes and looked up into

his astonished face. Her voice slurred and unsteady she got out, 'We—we in London yet?'

'London?' He looked even more amazed, then his voice became grim as he said curtly, 'No, we're not near London. We're in the Atlantic Ocean heading for America!'

CHAPTER TWO

MICHELLE moaned miserably, feeling too ill to take in the real implication of his words and only aware that the terrible voyage wasn't over yet and that the rotten boat was going to go on rolling and pitching indefinitely.

The owner seemed quite impervious to her pitiful condition; the amazed look had left his face, to be replaced by one of hard-eyed anger.

'How long have you been here? How did you get on board?' he demanded. Michelle could only groan in answer and he impatiently repeated, 'When did you come on board?'

'L-last . . .' She tried to tell him, but her stomach came up into her throat again and she had to put a hand over her mouth. 'F—feel sick.'

'Well, don't do it in here. Get out to the bathroom.'

He reached to pull down the sleeping bag and caught hold of her arm, none too gently, intending to pull her on to her feet, but then his startled eyes took in her nakedness and he said, 'Good God!' for a second time. For a moment he seemed nonplussed, but then the boat rolled even farther than usual and Michelle groped wildly for the edge of the bunk, her eyes desperate.

'Hang on!' he commanded curtly, and disappeared out of the cabin while she fought desperately to control her heaving insides. Within a minute he was back with a navy-blue towelling bathrobe. 'Here, put this on.'

Michelle groped for it and tried to put it on inside the bag, still keeping one hand over her mouth, but the man gave an impatient exclamation and she suddenly found herself lifted bodily from the bed and the robe being wrapped round her, then she was picked up in a pair of strong arms, carried the few yards to the bathroom and deposited on the floor with her head over the loo.

Above her she heard him swear and mutter, 'Damn this storm,' but Michelle was too busy being sick to care about him or anything else.

He must have left her almost immediately, because when she had recovered enough to look round she was grateful to find that she was alone. Somehow she managed to crawl back across the heaving, rolling floor to the bunk and climb in it, feeling more wretched than she had ever done in her life and praying with every ounce of faith she possessed for the boat to stay still and for her to be able to get out and on to dry land.

But the boat went on corkscrewing about for hours, first up and down, then sideways, then both together, and twice more Michelle had to stagger to the bathroom until there was nothing left in her stomach and she just retched horribly, which was worse than being sick. She fell over, too, as she tried to keep her balance, and banged her hip badly against the door jamb but felt so ill that she hardly noticed the pain, it was just part and parcel of the whole ghastly experience.

At some point she was dimly aware of the man coming back into the cabin and leaning over her. He lifted her head up and made her drink something. She didn't want to and tried to push it away, but he was insistent and she obeyed him because she had no strength left to resist. The liquid made her cough and choke at first and it stung her throat as it went down, but afterwards she could feel it warm in her chest and her stomach didn't feel quite so bad, so that she was able to fall into an uneasy, exhausted sleep.

The blissful awareness that the boat was comparatively still, just moving gently with the swell, was the first thing that penetrated to her mind and stomach when she awoke some hours later. Gingerly she sat up, fully expecting to have to dive out to the bathroom again, but apart from a clawing, empty sensation her stomach didn't feel too bad. It was daylight again, when she drew the curtains back the sun flooded into the cabin and sent dust motes dancing in the air.

Leaning back against the wall of the cabin, she looked down at the bathrobe and tried to remember what had happened. Her hangover seemed to have disappeared with the seasickness and her head didn't ache any more, just felt thick and cotton-woolly. Now she could recall vividly her quarrel with Peter and her fall into the river. She wondered how long he had looked for her before he had given up. Serve him right, she thought angrily, remembering how he'd tried to make her drunk so that he could take her. But then, in all fairness, he too had had quite a bit to drink, and, even to her somewhat limited experience, she knew that usually a boy's libido increased in direct proportion with his alcoholic intake. Not that it ever seemed to be far from the surface anyway: in the year since she had left school and been going out with boys she seemed to have spent most of her time fighting them off and refusing to go to bed with them. Although, when most of the boys she'd dated still lived at home with their parents, bed was usually the last place in which they tried to seduce a girl; it was more often the back seat of a car, up against a wall in a dark lane, in a lonely field, or—most dangerous of all—on a settee after their parents had gone to bed. Going steady with Peter had had the same problems, but he had been easier to handle than some of the others and she had been able to hold him off by making promises for the future; a promise he'd wasted no time at all in trying to make her keep, she recalled resentfully.

She wondered what he was doing now and what everyone at the party's reaction would be when he rushed in and said she'd fallen in the river. As the child of very famous parents she was used to always having to take a back seat, and it rather pleased her that she should be the centre of attention for a while, even if she wasn't there to see it. It occurred to her that they might even have thought that she was drowned. After all, no one knew that she'd managed to get aboard this boat. And it must have sailed from the Thames soon after, so even if they'd thought she might be on a boat they wouldn't have found her. A satisfied grin came to Michelle's mouth as she dwelt on the scene in her imagination. She could just picture Peter's parents telephoning her mother with the dreadful news. Here the smile faded as she cynically realised that her mother would make full theatrical use of the situation, getting as much free publicity out of it as possible and acting the part of the distraught parent as only she knew how. And of course she would insist on carrying on with the opening of her new play despite the agony of mind she was going through. The show must go on. She couldn't disappoint her public, and all the other stock, meaningless phrases. Michelle's mouth twisted bitterly. God, her mother would love every minute of it! And how chagrined she'd be when her lost, drowned daughter turned up safe and sound after all. But she'd rise above it, she always did. She would just go into her rapturous, adoring mother routine when anyone was around and switch it off immediately they were alone, knowing full well that her charm no longer worked on Michelle.

Sitting up in the bunk, she tried to work out how long she had been on the boat and how long it would take to get back to London. Obviously it must be into the second day now, but she had no idea at all how long it would take to get back, but her disappearance must have created quite a stir already. Perhaps they might even have sent for her father. But he was on location somewhere and in the middle of shooting a film, so whether he would be able or willing to fly to England was debatable. He was, she judged, fond of her in his own way and she had always wanted to visit him and the two wives he had got through since her mother, but Adele Verlaine had always let her know that he didn't want Michelle living with him permanently.

A great welling bitterness filled her heart at their neglect of her, the need for love that they had never fulfilled. Serve them right if she didn't come back at all, she thought malevolently, or at least not for quite some time. Enough time for them to feel remorseful of their treatment of her.

The more Michelle let that idea run round in her mind the better she liked it. And after all, why not? What was it the man had said? That they were heading for America? If she could somehow persuade him to take her with him instead of back to England ... For a moment the misery of the stormy night filled her mind and she almost rejected the idea, but with the optimism and speed of recovery of the young she was able to push the whole ghastly episode out of her mind, confident that it couldn't happen again. The biggest problem, of course, would be to persuade the owner not to take her back to London. But what if the news of her disappearance was announced over the radio; would he put two and two together and take her straight back? Not that he was to know that she'd boarded the boat in London, though, for all he knew she could have got on when he was tied up in Calais. Perhaps she could even pretend to be French or something so that he wouldn't suspect her real identity?

She'd got that far in her reasoning when there was an imperative rap on the door and it was immediately pushed open as the man came in. For a brief second Michelle thought of feigning sleep to give herself more time to think, but he came in so quickly that there was no time to slide down into the sleeping-bag.

'So you're awake, are you?' He came and stood beside the bunk, looking down at her grimly. 'How do you feel?'

Michelle gulped, then took the plunge and said in what she hoped was a broken French accent, 'Much better, *m'sieur*, *merci*.'

His brows drew together slightly as he looked at her intently for a moment. Then, 'Are you hungry?'

To Michelle's surprise she found she was. '*Oui, m'sieur.*'

'Then get up and fix yourself something—there's food in the galley.'

She looked at him indignantly. 'But I 'ave no clothes!'

'Then come as you are,' he answered unsympathetically.

'But—but, please, couldn't you bring me something, *m'sieur*?'

His dark eyes grew cold and his voice hardened. 'If you want to eat, you'll have to get it. I'm not acting as steward for a damned stowaway. And hurry up about it—you've got a whole lot of explainng to do.' He moved towards the door and then looked back. 'And wash your face, you look a mess.'

Michelle glared at him indignantly; who the hell did he think he was, giving her orders like that? But her stomach was making noises and the thought of food drew her like a magnet. Going into the bath-room she looked in the mirror and grimaced. She saw what he meant; her mascara was still smudged round her eyes and there were streaks of tar on her cheek which must have come from the river. Her hair, too, was a tangled, dishevelled mess.

Getting her face clean was easy, but she didn't know what to do about her hair until she realised that a leather toilet case had been put in the built-in cupboard. Michelle felt no compunction about using the brush and comb she found inside it; if the man wanted her to be tidy then he would have to supply the means. Her underwear was dry enough to put on now, but even so she instinctively wrapped the bathrobe tighter round herself as she padded bare-foot out to the galley.

The owner was already there. What was it the French Customs man had called him? Yes, Farringdon, that was it. He was making coffee, the smell of which almost made Michelle drool. She'd never felt so hungry in her life. He looked round as she came in and his eyes widened in surprise.

'Quite a transformation! You look about ten years younger. Just how old are you, anyway?'

'I 'ave nine ... twenty-four years, *m'sieur*,' Michelle amended hastily, thinking that the older she made herself out to be the better. She looked at the partly cut long French loaf lying on the worktop and her mouth watered. 'May I?' She gestured towards it.

'Go ahead.' He poured out two mugs of coffee and carried them to the nearby table, sitting down and watching her while she hacked off a large chunk of bread and spread it thickly with the butter and smoked ham left beside the loaf.

Michelle sat down opposite him, aware of him watching her, but so hungry that she completely ignored him until she'd eaten her sandwich and drunk her coffee. Then she sat back, licking her lips, and found his dark grey eyes watching her with a slightly amused look in their depths.

'Feeling better?'

She nodded. 'Yes, th—*merci, m'sieur.*'

'Good.' He had been sitting back in his seat, smoking a cigarette, but now he stubbed it out and leant forward, the amusement in his eyes replaced by a cool intentness. 'So now you've got some explaining to do, young lady. Just how did you get on my boat, and why?'

A chill of nervousness ran through her and Michelle stammered a little as she answered, 'It—it was at Calais, *m'sieur.*' Fervently she wished she'd had more time to work out some story to tell him, some reason for her to have boarded his boat in broad daylight that he would believe. As it was, all she could think of was to stick near the truth. 'I—I had been to a party; on another boat, you understand? And I fell into the ri . . . the sea, and the tide carried me to your boat. I called but no one came, so I . . .'

'Just a minute,' he interrupted her brusquely. 'This party—when did it start?'

Michelle wrinkled her forehead, desperately trying

to work it out, then her brow cleared; the truth would do again. 'On the sixteenth, *m'sieur*. It was a long party, you understand? It went on all night and the next day. It was daylight when I fell in the water.'

'What was the name of the boat?'

A blank look came into her face. 'I—I do not know. I went to it with some other people.'

He nodded, apparently accepting the statement, and Michelle gave an inner sigh of relief.

'How did you fall in?'

'I am afraid I was a little—how do you say it?—a little tipsy and . . .'

'Drunk,' he interrupted laconically.

Michelle glared at him. 'A little tipsy,' she repeated firmly, 'and I tripped over a rope.'

'And no one heard you cry for help?'

'No. No one. I was very frightened. I thought I would drown, *m'sieur*. But then I came near your boat and I caught hold of the rope and pulled myself up on board.' She smiled at him, enjoying herself now. 'It was most fortunate, was it not?'

'Oh, most,' Farringdon agreed sardonically. 'And I suppose that by now your friends will have reported you missing?'

'Oh, no,' Michelle told him blithely. 'I didn't really know anyone there. It was an open party, anyone could go. No one will miss me.'

The dark eyes narrowed again. 'I see. It's strange, I didn't hear the noise of a party on any of the boats anchored near mine.'

'It was not so noisy then, *m'sieur*. And the boat was some distance from yours.'

'Really? You were lucky, then. When no one on the boat saw you go in, and no one—even with all the shipping in Calais harbour—saw you in the water, and that evening dress that you have hanging in the cabin weighing you down; why, you were extremely lucky not to have drowned.'

'*Mais oui, m'sieur.*'

Pleased that he was accepting her story so readily, Michelle hadn't noticed the coldness that had entered his voice until he suddenly shot out a hand, gripped her wrist where it lay on the table, and bit out, 'What's your name?'

'Mich . . .' She faltered in her automatic response, suddenly aware that that was the last thing she wanted him to know.

But he was watching her keenly, his eyes alert and penetrating. 'Go on,' he commanded curtly, 'Mich . . . Michelle?'

Slowly, nervously, she nodded, trying hard not to let her hand shake in his grasp.

'Michelle . . . what?'

A name from her old French textbooks at school came providentially to mind. 'Monet,' she answered. 'Michelle Monet.' She tried to look him in the face as she said it, but his eyes were boring into hers and she flushed and looked away.

Immediately the grip on her wrist tightened. Silkily he said, 'That was a very amusing story, *mademoiselle*, but now I think we'll have the truth.'

Alarmed, she tried to brazen it out. 'I 'ave told you the truth, *m'sieur*. Every word is . . . Oh!' She broke off as he slowly and deliberately began to twist her wrist. '*M'sieur*, you are 'urting me! D—don't! Stop it!' But he didn't take any notice, just continued to twist until she was on her feet, crying out and trying vainly to prise his fingers off her wrist. 'Stop it, d'you hear me? Let me go!' She was yelling now, the French accent completely forgotten.

Suddenly he did let go, a sardonic curve to his

mouth as Michelle stood and rubbed he
wrist. 'You beast! How dare you hurt me like t
Just because I got on your rotten . . .' She broke on
aware of what she was saying and the way he was
looking at her. 'Oh!'

'Quite. And now that we've got rid of the phoney
accent maybe we can have the true story.'

Slowly she sat down again, looking at him resentfully. 'How did you know?'

'You spoke to me in the night when you were
ill, and although it was only a few words they certainly weren't in French. If you hadn't known you
were on an English boat you would have spoken in
French.'

'Oh.' She looked at him nervously, wondering
what to tell him.

'I'm waiting,' he reminded her drily.

'Well,' frantically she tried to think of something,
'what I told you was partly true. I—I had been to a
party.' Inspiration suddenly came. 'In Calais. I'd
gone over there for the weekend. I was with a man,
and I was going to spend the night with him,' she
added brazenly, trying to ignore the swift, specu-
lative look he gave her. 'But—well, he got drunk
and—and offensive, and I changed my mind. We
had a row when I wouldn't sleep with him and he
locked me out of the hotel room so that I couldn't
change or get my things. I slept on a chair in the
corridor all night and waited till the next morning,
but he must have been out cold, because he didn't
open the door when I banged on it.'

She hesitated and gave the boat owner a quick
look under her lashes, but he was still watching her
narrowly and she plunged on, 'Well, then it got
embarrassing. People were starting to get up and I
didn't want to be found there, so I walked down to

the harbour. I had some idea of getting a lift back to
England in one of the cars going over on the ferry,
but I didn't have any money or my passport or anything, so no one would take me. But then I met a
local boy who said there were a lot of English boats
in the harbour, so he rowed me out here and I
sneaked on board.'

'You saw me leave the boat?'

Uneasily she nodded, not knowing what to say for
the best.

'So you intended to stow away—to stay hidden
until we got back to England?'

'Yes. I—I'm sorry.' She opened her eyes wide and
looked at him appealingly, something she'd often
seen her mother do. But she couldn't have been
doing it right, because it seemed to have entirely the
wrong effect on this man.

'You're sorry,' he sneered derisively. 'And I suppose you expect me to just accept your apology and
turn round and take you back to London? Well, it
isn't quite as simple as that. I left France in an all-
fired hurry because I've already left it to the last
minute to keep an appointment in the West Indies.
My crewman went sick and I was trying to find a
replacement, but in the end had to sail without one.
Now, by having to turn round and take you back
I'm going to lose at least two days, probably three
by the time I've got it all sorted out and refuelled.
Legally, I suppose I ought to take you back to Calais
where I found you and dump you back into their
laps.'

Michelle looked at him cautiously, resenting being
referred to almost as an unwanted parcel but aware
that he had given her an opening. 'You don't have
to go back to London—or Calais—on my account.'

His head came up sharply. 'What's that supposed

to mean?'

She tried to shrug offhandedly. 'My time's my own. I wouldn't mind a trip to the West Indies. And you said you needed some help on the boat. Why don't I take the place of your crewman?'

The grey eyes had narrowed, were regarding her searchingly. 'Are you serious?'

'Yes. Why not?' Michelle tried to make her voice sound confident, but her heart was pumping loudly in her chest.

'Do you know anything about sailing?'

'Of course,' she lied. 'I've been on boats before.'

'Really? Then you'll know what a spring is?'

Michelle raised her eyebrows. What a stupid question. 'Of course I know what a spring is. It's a piece of metal shaped like a spiral.'

'And a warp?'

She looked at him suspiciously. 'It's a bit of wood that's bent out of shape—isn't it?' she added hesitantly.

He looked at her contemptuously. 'Well, now we both know that you know absolutely nothing about boating. A warp is the name we use for a rope and a spring is when we tie the warps diagonally from the boat to the bank or another boat to prevent them hitting. As crew you'd be absolutely useless. I'd be doing myself a favour to put you on the nearest point of land.'

'Oh, no, please. I know I could help, really I could. I could keep the boat clean and I could . . .' she sought for something that sounded remotely nautical, 'I could swab the decks,' she managed triumphantly.

His mouth twisted in wry amusement. 'Can you cook?'

'Oh, yes,' she agreed, much too fervently.

'Which probably means that that's a lie too and you can't even boil an egg.' Farringdon leaned back in his chair and regarded her through the smoke of his cigarette for a few moments while Michelle sat and fidgeted uneasily under his scrutiny. Abruptly he asked, 'What about your family, won't they have something to say about you going to America?'

'I haven't any family,' Michelle answered with bitter conviction. 'No one close enough to care if I go away for a while.'

'Are you running away from something or someone?'

Michelle's eyes widened in some surprise and she shook her head. 'No.' It hadn't occurred to her that that was what she was doing.

'Are you sure?' he demanded grimly.

Her chin came up. 'Quite sure.'

'What about your passport, I suppose your—er—boy-friend still has that?'

'What?' For a moment she was disconcerted, then remembered that she was supposed to have been with a man in Calais. 'Oh, yes. Well, that's no problem. I can send a telegram when we get to the West Indies asking him to send it on to me.'

'You have his address?'

She looked at him defiantly. 'Yes.'

He frowned and drew hard on his cigarette so that the end glowed red. 'Are you telling me the truth?'

Michelle put her hands under the table and crossed her fingers. 'Yes, of course I am.'

'If I wasn't so short of time I'd have no hesitation whatsoever in taking you back and handing you over, but as it is . . .' He continued to frown at her while Michelle waited in trepidation. 'As it is,' he repeated, his eyes running over her, 'I really don't have the time to spare. And you might be able to provide some creature comforts at that.'

He ground out his cigarette, the decision made. 'All right, I'll take you along. You can radio to your boy-friend for your passport over the boat's radio.' He stood up. 'What's your real name? I never heard anything so phoney as Michelle Monet in my life. So what were you really going to say?'

Michelle looked at him in annoyance, but said 'It's Mitchell.' Adding, 'June Mitchell,' after a quick look at a calendar on the wall for inspiration.

'Now that I believe.' He stood up and looked down at her. 'All right, June Mitchell, you've got yourself a job. Welcome aboard the *Ethos*,' he added sardonically, his tone far from welcoming. 'You can start by cleaning the place up.'

He went to go on deck again, but Michelle called after him. 'Wait! You haven't told me your name yet.'

He paused and looked back. 'So I haven't. It's Guy Farringdon.'

For a moment their eyes met and held, then Michelle gave a brief nod of acknowledgement and he turned and ran lightly up the steps.

CHAPTER THREE

As soon as he'd gone, Michelle dived across the galley to cut herself another sandwich and pour out a second cup of coffee. Even as she did so she heard the engine open out and the boat seemed to surge forward. Guy Farringdon making up for the time he'd lost while he was talking to her, she supposed. Fleetingly she wondered what appointment he could be making for in the West Indies that was so important, and which particular island, but she wasn't really worried; just glad that she had got her own way and would be out of touch for a few days. Long enough to put a scare into her parents and make them take some notice of her when she reappeared.

For a while she was afraid that she would feel sick again once the boat started moving, but it sailed smoothly over the sea, hardly rocking or rolling at all, and Michelle realised that it had only been the storm that had made it so unstable. She began to feel better and more cheerful by the minute and to look around her, taking in her new surroundings. The galley was beautifully equipped with a large upright deep-freeze cabinet as well as a refrigerator, both well stocked with food, and there was also a small washing machine and tumble dryer on top of one another near the sink. The cupboards, when she opened them, contained a large quantity of food and drink and there was a range of new-looking cooking utensils under the cooker. Everything one would need, in fact, for a fairly long voyage. And the boat, plus everything in it, looked brand new. Could this be some sort of maiden voyage Guy Farringdon was making? she wondered.

As instructed, she put away the rest of the food and then wiped down the working surfaces, rolling her sleeves up to stop them getting in the way. The bathrobe was much too big, reaching well down towards her feet, and went almost twice round her slim figure. She hoped that her new boss had some other clothes she could wear, because she certainly didn't want to spend the whole voyage dressed in this.

When she'd finished, she stood uncertainly, wondering what to do, but the sunshine streaming through the windows beckoned and she made her way up the steps to the large, airy saloon and then through a door on to the deck. Funny, she must have come through this way when she'd boarded the boat in London, but she couldn't remember a thing about it; she must have been far drunker than she'd realised.

As soon as she stepped into the open the breeze caught her hair and blew it about her head, whipping too at the skirts of the bathrobe and blowing them up round her hips. Pushing her hair out of her eyes with one hand and holding her skirts down with the other, she looked around for Farringdon but couldn't see him, then noticed a ladder with four steps leading up to the roof of the saloon. Gingerly she held on to the rails and climbed the steps. Guy Farringdon was seated in a swivel seat in front of a control panel with the wheel in his hands, steering the boat across the open sea. The wind was stronger up here and she found it difficult to hold the bathrobe down and keep her hair out of her eyes at the same time. She began to cross the few feet towards him, but just then the boat slapped into a wave and tilted to one side so that Michelle had to make a grab for the rail, the robe blowing open up to her waist.

Pushing her hair out of the way, she saw that Guy Farringdon was looking at her legs, his mouth twisted in appreciative amusement. Angrily she pulled the robe back into place and said coldly, 'I need some clothes.'

He grinned openly. 'So I see.' Turning, he did something to the levers on the control panel and then let go the wheel. 'Okay, let's see if I can find you something.'

He got out of the seat and went to go past her, but Michelle said nervously, 'What about the boat? Won't it go the wrong way with no one to steer it?'

An exasperated look came into the grey eyes. 'It's on auto-pilot. How else did you expect me to get across the Atlantic single-handed?' he demanded impatiently. 'I have to sleep some time.'

'I—I don't know. I didn't think about it.'

The exasperated look gave way to one of slight contempt, but he didn't say anything, just led the way down the ladder again and back through the boat to the single cabin at the front where she'd spent her first night. There was a big holdall on the floor there now, not yet unpacked, which he picked up and put on the bunk while he sorted through it.

'Here, try these.' He pulled out a navy blue sweater and a white tee-shirt, then a pair of denim jeans.

Michelle held the jeans against her. They were about a foot too long and the waist was several sizes too big. 'I'm going to need a belt.'

He fished in the bag again and gave her a narrow brown leather one. 'That will be too big as well. Put it round your waist and I'll mark it and punch a couple more holes in.'

Obediently Michelle put the belt round her slender waist, pulled the thong through the buckle and held it in place while he took a pen from his pocket and marked it. He came very close to her as he did so, casually resting one hand on her hip. Michelle caught the masculine, woody drift of his after-shave, all mixed up with the tangy sea smells of his sweater. He seemed very big up so close, at least six feet two, and his shoulders proportionately broad and well-muscled. He was big, tough and supremely self-confident, and for the first time it occurred to her that she had placed herself in the hands of a complete stranger, an unknown man who would be her sole companion for the next few days. She stirred uneasily, realising that she'd been so caught up in the idea of teaching her parents a lesson that she had looked on Guy Farringdon as just a means to an end, not as a person at all.

When she moved the hold on her hip tightened. 'Keep still,' he commanded. 'There, that should be about right.' Taking a large pen-knife from his pocket, the type that has about a dozen different blades and tools, he deftly pushed holes through the marks he'd made. 'Try that.'

'It's fine,' she assured him, fastening it. 'Thanks.' She went to move away, but he stopped her.

'Here, I'll cut off the end for you. No, don't bother to take it off.' He sawed through the leather with his knife, his head bent so that it was quite close to hers. Michelle moved her head away and he glanced quickly up at her, a slight frown coming between his eyes, but then she gave him a quick, nervous smile and he went on with his task.

As soon as he'd finished she picked up the clothes.

'I'll go and change.' Without looking at him she went into the cabin she'd been using and shut the door, then hesitated a moment before sliding the bolt across. It wasn't that she didn't trust Guy Farringdon, but she had suddenly become aware of him as a member of the opposite sex and somehow felt safer with the door locked.

The clothes of course were far too big and hung on her like sacks. The tee-shirt wasn't too bad because she could tuck it into the belted waist of the jeans, but the legs were miles too long; she had to roll them up several times before her feet appeared at the bottom. Looking at herself in the mirror, Michelle groaned aloud; she looked like some barefoot orphan waif dressed in cast-off clothes that she was expected to grow into. She looked terrible! Well, they would have to do. And perhaps it wouldn't be too bad an idea to look terrible anyway; from her limited experience she knew that the more glamorous you looked the more boy-friends tried to make a pass, therefore the reverse must also hold good; the uglier you looked the less likely they were to try anything. And somehow she had the feeling that the less attractive she appeared to Guy Farringdon the better.

He was nowhere around when she ventured out of the cabin, probably up at the controls again, she guessed, so she took the opportunity to explore the big saloon on the deck above. It was very luxurious with a big soft semi-circular seat set round a fixed coffee table, with a couple more upholstered seats, a built-in stereo system and a large, but empty, cocktail bar. The bookshelves under one window were also empty, as were the cupboards for records and cassettes. Michelle frowned in puzzlement, wondering why he hadn't bothered to bring any leisure entertainment with him. But the whole boat was obviously very new, perhaps he just hadn't had time to equip it properly since he'd bought it.

For a while she sat and looked out of the window, but soon became bored by the endless vista of unbroken sea and went below to the galley again. Opening a door she hadn't yet explored, Michelle found herself in yet another sleeping cabin, a large double one, not with bunks in it, but with a large double bed with rounded off corners. There was also a built-in settee under one window as well as a dressing-table-cum-desk and a couple of wardrobes, but what really made Michelle's eyebrows go up was the small but compact bathroom opening off it, and which she worked out must be alongside the unwindowed wall of the galley. Everything was very luxurious, very beautifully designed and made, with obvious care and attention being lavished on every detail to get it right.

For several minutes Michelle just stood staring round the room, wondering why on earth Guy Farringdon should choose for himself a small, single cabin right up in the front of the boat when he could use this comparatively huge and airy one instead. After a while she shrugged and gave it up; perhaps he would tell her some time during the voyage.

Restlessly, she went back to her own cabin, but there was nothing to hold her attention there and she began to feel increasingly bored. There didn't even seem to be anything on the boat to read. Then she remembered the books she'd seen on a shelf in Guy Farringdon's cabin; perhaps there would be something there that would interest her.

His cabin backed on to hers and she quickly pushed open the door and went inside. It was as he'd left it, with the clothes partly unpacked from his holdall and left on the bed. Mostly they were working clothes, jeans and sweaters, but there were also a couple of pairs of shorts and a pair of brief white swimming trunks, ready for the hotter weather of the West Indies presumably. She looked at the book titles, but then sighed with disappointment; they were all nautical books about boats, sea-lore or sea voyages, nothing to interest her at all. Turning to go, the white trunks again caught her eye. They were really awfully brief, and for a moment she couldn't help imagining what Guy Farringdon's big frame would look like in nothing but them. A strange sensation flickered through her and she shivered, then suddenly jumped in fright as the door was pulled abruptly open and the real man stood in front of her, a thunderous look on his face.

'What the hell are you doing in here?'

'I—I . . .' Somehow Michelle managed to conquer her fright and stutter, 'I was looking for a book to read.'

'A book? Just what do you think this is—a leisure cruise?' he demanded angrily. 'I told you to clean the place up.'

'I did,' Michelle retorted indignantly. 'I put the food away and wiped down the worktop.'

'So what happened to the rest of the boat?' Guy pursued, his anger in no way abated. 'I took you on as a member of the crew, remember? And no way are you going to sit about reading when there's work to be done.'

'All right,' Michelle retorted, her own temper rising, 'I get the message. If you'll just tell me what you want me to do, then I'll do it.'

His face hardened. 'Look around you, open your eyes. The bathroom is in a mess, there are several cases of stores in the galley that need stowing away, and the deck in there needs washing down too. Your own cabin needs airing, and while you're in here you can finish unpacking my gear. And when you've done that,' he added curtly, 'you can start cooking some lunch.'

Michelle glared at him, infuriated by his patronising tone. 'Yes, Captain,' she answered insolently. 'Anything you say, Captain.'

The grey eyes narrowed dangerously. 'Just watch it,' he warned her softly, and suddenly the anger left her and she was afraid.

'I—I'm sorry. I didn't know what you wanted me to do.'

For a few seconds longer he continued to look at her intently, then he nodded. 'All right. But just remember that I'm not carrying any passengers on this trip, you're going to have to work your passage, one way or the other.'

'Yes, all right.' She lowered her head and didn't lift it again until he'd gone. To her annoyance she found that she was shaking. The horrible man! How dared he yell at her like that? He'd only got to tell her what he wanted her to do, hadn't he? But all the same she immediately began to unpack the rest of his things and put them away in the drawers and locker, working as quickly as she could. The bathroom she found harder to do, because always there had been maids to clear up after her at home and she'd never had to clean a room before in her life. By the time she'd finished her arms ached and she was hungry again, but she still hadn't even started putting away the stores in the galley, let alone washing down the floor in there.

Half an hour later she was on her knees in the galley, a cloth in her hand, giving the floor a cursory wipe over, when she was almost startled out of her wits by a shrill, piercing sound and then Guy's voice, the tone rather echoey and seeming to come from mid-air, demanded, 'Mitch? Are you in there?'

For a moment Michelle couldn't think what was happening or who he was speaking to, then realised that he must have shortened the false name of June Mitchell that she'd given him to Mitch. But where was his voice coming from? Standing up, she looked wildly round, but then his voice, impatient this time, came again.

'The communication console is built into the bulkhead on the port side. You press the button marked "SPEAK" and hold it down while you answer.'

Completely disconcerted and hardly understanding a word of what he'd said, Michelle searched hastily round the cabin. What on earth was a bulkhead? And which was the port side? Then, mercifully, she caught sight of the 'SPEAK' button among several others grouped together under what looked like a small speaker set into the wall above and to the left of the fridge. She'd noticed it before but had thought it was a radio or cassette player. Hastily she pressed the button. 'Yes, I'm here.'

There was no reply and she looked at the speaker in puzzlement until she realised that she was still pressing in the knob. She took her finger off immediately and just caught the last few syllables of what Guy had been saying. Unhappily she pressed the knob again. 'I'm afraid I didn't quite catch that.'

This time she remembered to remove her finger and his voice came through quite clearly. 'I said I have to radio in in ten minutes. Come to the wheelhouse on the main deck then and give me the name and address of your boy-friend so that we can have your passport sent on.'

He stopped speaking and Michelle pressed the

button. 'Er—which is the main deck?'

Even through the communicator she could hear the resigned note in his voice. 'The main deck is the one above your head. The wheelhouse is behind the saloon. You get to it from a sliding door on the starboard side of the deck.' He paused, then added, 'How's lunch coming along?'

'Oh! Oh, fine,' she lied heartily.

'Good. We'll have it as soon as I've finished on the radio.'

'Yes, all right.'

Hurriedly Michelle opened cupboards and pulled out some tins. Potatoes, peas, carrots; yes, they would do. And in the freezer she found a couple of lamb chops. But then came the difficult part, she had to light the gas and nowhere could she find any matches, no matter how she searched.

'Oh!' In angry frustration she banged shut cupboards and drawers, going over the same ground twice in her hurry. There just had to be matches, or how could you light the gas? An idea suddenly occurred to her and she experimentally turned one of the gas taps. The ring immediately popped into blazing life and she saw now that there was a pilot light on the cooker. She groaned in annoyance, then hastily put the chops under the grill, turning the gas up high so that they would cook quickly. There was a tin opener in the cutlery drawer, and after several minutes in which she swore more than once, she managed to hack the tins of vegetables open enough to pour out the contents into a saucepan, mixing them all up together. After all, they all went down the same way, didn't they?

She'd hardly finished before Guy's voice came over the speaker again. 'I said ten minutes. Why aren't you up here?'

Damn the man, did he have to be so impatient? Leaving the food to cook, she ran up the steps to the deck and hurried towards the front of the boat past the windows of the saloon. Now which side had he said? More by luck than judgement she found the sliding door and saw Guy through the window. Pushing the door open, she went inside and found him sitting in front of a wheel similar to that on the open deck above, but here there were far more gadgets and levers, none of which meant a thing to her except what looked like an extremely modern and efficient radio set fixed on to the wall on Guy's left.

He didn't acknowledge her arrival at all, just picked up a hand microphone and spoke into it. 'This is *Ethos* calling Farringdon One. Do you receive me? Over.'

The radio set crackled a little with static and Guy moved the tuner round the dial a fraction. Then an answering voice said, 'This is Farringdon One to *Ethos*. Receiving you loud and clear. How's it going? Over.'

Guy replied, 'Fine, so far. There was quite a storm last night, but she weathered it like a dream.' For a few moments he gave some technical information including their present position to the voice at the end of the radio waves, then added, 'By the way, I took on a crew member at the last minute who needs a passport sent on. I want you to get in touch with the address I give you and ask them to send the passport for J. Mitchell, repeat J. Mitchell, by airmail to the main post office in Hamilton, Bermuda to await collection. Tell them to address the envelope to me so that I can pick it up. Got that?' He waited for an affirmative, then went on, 'Okay, the address is . . .' he looked at Michelle enquiringly and she blithely gave him an entirely fictitious name and

address which he duly repeated into the microphone.

She smiled secretly to herself as he did so; to have
given the correct address would have meant an
immediate end to the game she was playing, but this
way she would be safe until they landed in Bermuda
and he found that her passport hadn't arrived at the
post office. What Guy Farringdon's reaction might
be then she decided to put off thinking about, knowing instinctively that he wouldn't like it one little
bit.

He talked for a few moments more, then turned off
the radio set.

'Who were you speaking to?' she asked him curiously.

'The manager of my boatyard near Gravesend.'

'*Your* boatyard?'

He glanced at her briefly. 'That's right. I build
boats, sea cruisers mainly. And this beauty is the
first off the production line of our newest model.' He
put out a hand to the spokes of the wooden steering
wheel as he said it, and touched them caressingly,
lovingly almost, a distinct note of pride in his voice.

'And this trip—are you testing out the boat?'

Guy shook his head. 'No, she's already undergone
all her sea trials. This voyage is purely business; I
hope to get orders from several brokers in the West
Indies and also at the Miami boat show next
month.'

'Will there be many other boats there?'

'Hundreds, I should think.'

'How do you know you'll get any orders, then?'

'I don't,' he answered briefly, only giving her
question half his attention as he wrote up the boat's
log-book. 'But she's a good boat. We've put everything we've got into her. Everyone in the yard broke

their backs to try and get her ready in time to ship over by cargo boat, but we were held up for one or two vital parts for the steering gear and were just too late, so I decided to sail her over to the States myself.'

'Aren't the boats usually sailed across, then?' Michelle asked him.

'No, as I said, they're usually shipped across. Even a boat this size is small for the Atlantic.' He finished writing and put the book down, turning to look at her fully. 'Scared?'

Frowning, she shook her head. 'No—I don't know. Should I be?'

'One should always be in awe of the sea. It can play strange tricks.' He stood up, his head almost brushing the roof of the cabin. 'Let's have lunch.'

Michelle turned to precede him out on to the deck, then paused. 'Why are there two steering wheels?'

'The boat has dual controls, so that you can control her from here when the weather is wet or rough or up on the flying bridge when it's fine. Personally I prefer to be out in the open on the flying bridge whenever I can.'

They began to walk along the deck towards the door leading to the galley, but had only gone a few feet before a strong smell of burning reached their nostrils.

'What the hell . . .?' Guy pushed her unceremoniously out of the way and sprang for the steps.

Michelle went to run after him, but stopped precipitately as his bellow of rage from the galley made her suddenly realise what the smell was. Oh, God, she'd forgotten the chops! For a moment she hesitated, afraid to face him and ready to make herself scarce until he'd cooled off, but before she could do so, Guy reached up through the doorway and pulled her willy-nilly down the steps.

'You crazy idiot! Look what you've done!'

He'd turned the gas taps off, but the galley and the corridor leading to the front cabins were full of smoke from the chops which had burnt to a cinder. The water in the vegetables, too, had evaporated and there was just a burnt, dried-up mess in the bottom of the brand new saucepan. Disgustedly he slid open the window above the cooker and stuck the saucepan in the sink to fill it with water.

He looked at Michelle, his jaw tight with anger, and she found herself quaking with fright. 'Clean it up,' he gritted. 'But first make me a sandwich and some coffee and bring it up to the bridge. You can *make* coffee?' he tacked on, his tone infinitely sarcastic.

'Yes, of course I can. It's just that I'm not used to a gas cooker. I didn't know it would cook so quickly,' she added defensively.

His eyebrows rose rather sceptically, but he didn't say anything else, just left her to clean up the mess.

It took her ages, working away with the pot-scourer up to her elbows in filthy water until both the grill and the saucepan were shining clean again.

Afterwards she looked ruefully at her nails which had been long and beautifully manicured only a few hours ago; now the pink nail-varnish was chipped and flaking and there was a catch in one of them that needed filing. Ugh! Tiredly she sat down with a cup of coffee, but hadn't even finished it before Guy was calling her over the intercom with more jobs for her to do. All afternoon she worked, moving some stores from one side of the boat to the other because he said the trim wasn't right, or something equally stupid, and then it was time to cook another meal which she managed not to burn only by standing by and watching it anxiously. That she'd managed it at all gave her quite a sense of achievement and in no way prepared her for the derisory look Guy gave to the meal when she placed his plate in front of him.

'Is that it?' he demanded after taking in the small boil-in-the-bag piece of fish in mushroom sauce, the few tinned potatoes and tablespoonful of peas.

'Why, yes.' Michelle looked at him in surprise. *Now* what was the matter?

'What's for dessert?'

'There—there isn't one.'

'I thought as much.' Putting his elbows on the table he leaned towards her. 'Have you ever cooked for a man before?'

Warily she shook her head. 'No, as a matter of fact I haven't.'

'That's pretty obvious. The meal you've given me would hardly keep a mouse alive, let alone a grown man. I get hungry up there on the bridge. I could eat this three times over. In future I want a decent-sized main course with soup first and a dessert to follow, then cheese and biscuits and real coffee, not the instant stuff you gave me at lunchtime. Understand?'

Michelle nodded in scarcely concealed anger mixed up with dismay. It had taken all her ingenuity to produce this meal, how on earth was she to manage all that he demanded? What did he think she was, a Cordon Bleu cook or something?

They ate the meal in virtual silence and Michelle reluctantly had to admit to herself that she, too, was still hungry after it. Not that she let him see, of course; instead she sat back in her seat as if she was full up and couldn't eat another bite. Guy looked at her sardonically and made her make up the last of the French bread and ham into a sandwich, which he took with a mug of coffee up to the bridge again. Michelle watched him go rather malevolently; she had been hoping to fill up on the bread herself, but instead she had to make do with a packet of chocolate biscuits she found in a cupboard.

Tiredly, then, she stood at the sink to wash the dishes, looking abstractedly out of the window at the slowly darkening sky. Her thoughts were miles away; on her mother mostly, wondering what she was doing and whether she had sent for her father, but then her thoughts came sharply back to the present as her attention was caught and held by the glow of the sunset. Uncluttered by hills and houses as it would be on land, the horizon lay stretched out in a long, seemingly endless line, and in the west, where sea and sky met, the brilliant colours were mirrored in the water, reflected and polished by the shimmering effect of the moving sea until they became almost too dazzling for the naked eye. Catching her breath in wonder, almost afraid to move in case she broke the spell, Michelle stood and gazed, her eyes opening wide to drink in and hold the glory of the scene that was unfolding before her. It was a fantastically beautiful sky, no lesser words could describe it, no adequate ones had yet been invented. The sky was blood-red on the lip of the horizon, turning to fluorescent pink at the edges of the feathered clouds that stroked the clear, deep blue of the upper stratosphere.

Slowly, as the sun sank behind the horizon, the other colours too disappeared, until the last of the light had gone and Michelle came back to reality to find herself standing in darkness, her hands still in the washing up water that had turned cold while she watched. The transition was not a pleasant one and she sighed as she turned on the light and finished the dishes. She felt incredibly tired after her night of seasickness and all the work she'd done today, and she longed for sleep.

The tempo of the engines changed as darkness fell and the boat slowed down, rolling a little more with the waves without the added speed to push her through them. Guy came into the galley soon afterwards, running a hand rather wearily down his face, and Michelle realised that he hadn't had much sleep during the storm last night either. Less than she'd had, probably.

'Make me a hot milk drink, would you? I'm bushed.'

Resentment prickled through her at the arrogant way he ordered her about, but he looked so weary that she silently took a packet of milk from the fridge and poured it into a saucepan, turning on the gas underneath.

'How do you manage to get any sleep when there's only you to drive the boat?' she asked him.

'I told you, there's an auto-pilot.'

'Oh, yes, of course.' Taking a big mug from a cupboard, she added powdered chocolate, but paused with the spoon in mid-air as a thought occurred to her. 'But what if another ship should run into us in the dark?'

'We're showing lights. And it's a big ocean. And anyway, we're not on a shipping lane.'

Michelle turned to stare at him in consternation. 'But what if a big tanker, or a liner or something, were to be off course? They'd never see our lights—we're too low in the water. They would run us down without even noticing.' Her voice rose in horror as she saw the whole scene in her imagination.

Guy grinned tiredly. 'It's all right, you don't have to worry. This boat is fitted with all the latest electronic gear available. She has a radar set that lets out a warning signal if anything comes within five miles when we're on auto.'

'What sort of warning signal?' Michelle demanded, not yet convinced.

'It sounds like an air-raid siren, an alarm clock and a girl screaming, all rolled into one. At the moment it's switched through to here, but when I turn in I'll switch it over to the crew's cabin.'

'You're sure it will wake you?'

'It'll wake the dead,' he assured her with a yawn. Then, 'The milk! It's boiling over.'

Hastily Michelle turned to grab the pan, but she'd forgotten the open tin of chocolate powder and her arm caught it and sent it flying. 'Oh, no!'

For a moment she was completely confused, trying to pick up the tin which had fallen on to the cooker with one hand, and the pan with the other, but the handle was so hot that she dropped it again and more milk splashed on to the flames, to hiss and bubble, the acrid smell filling the galley.

The next minute she was pushed out of the way as Guy turned off the gas, grabbed a cloth and lifted off the pan and righted the upset tin of powder. He looked at the state of the cooker and the pan and then turned on her, his tone scathing. 'You,' he told her, 'are the most useless, clumsy, landlubberly female it has ever been my misfortune to meet. Not only do you not know one end of a boat from the other, but you can't cook, can't clean, and are so damn hamfisted that you make more work than you do. If we ever manage to get to Bermuda in one piece,' he added through gritted teeth, 'I shall be very much surprised. Because the way you're going on you'll either set fire to the boat or blow us to kingdom come before you're through!'

Then he turned, poured what was left of the milk into the mug, and thrust the dirty pan into her hands. 'I'm turning in. Clean the mess up and put this in to soak overnight. Then *you* can turn in. And don't try skimping on the job,' he added curtly, 'because I'll check on it in the morning.'

He waited for her to speak, but she just stood and glared at him resentfully, very close to tears, her mouth set into a petulant, sulky line.

'Goodnight,' he said, and when she didn't answer shrugged his shoulders scornfully and walked out of the galley.

It was a good half an hour later before Michelle got to bed, but even though she was so tired she couldn't get to sleep. She lay listening to the creaking noises that the boat made and the sound of the waves slapping against the hull. It was such an alien environment, different from anything she had ever known before, and the thought of the smallness of the boat and the depth of water underneath the keel made her nervous. When the wind increased she was sure it was the sound of a ship's engines, and, when a particularly large wave hit the side, that it was the wash of a big ship close by. For what seemed like hours she lay tossing and turning uneasily in the bunk, until utter exhaustion made her fall asleep at last.

It seemed only two minutes later when she was woken by a loud banging on her door and Guy's voice calling her to get up.

'Come on! It's six-thirty and I want my breakfast. You can make it while I shower.'

Dazedly, her eyes hardly in focus, Michelle stumbled out of the bunk, then realised what he'd said. Six-thirty! Heavens, she'd never been up that early before in her life. Almost she rebelled and got back into bed, but the thought of his anger and contempt if she did made her put on his jeans and sweater and go yawningly into the galley, rubbing her eyes and looking at the cooking hob with a glazed expression as she tried to think what she was supposed to give him to eat.

Down the corridor behind her she could hear Guy whistling above the noise of the shower; evidently *he* had slept well and was feeling bright and refreshed, whereas Michelle looked out at where the cold grey vastness of the sea met an equally grey sky and shivered as she thought longingly of the warmth of her sleeping-bag.

Guy's hair was still damp when he came into the galley dressed in his usual jeans and Aran-knit sweater. He bade her a cheerful 'Good morning,' but Michelle's reply was muffled by a yawn.

'What's the matter—didn't you sleep well?' He put a casual hand up to brush a lock of damp hair off his forehead and sat down at the table.

'No,' Michelle answered grumpily, 'I didn't.'

Guy looked at the sullen set of her mouth and remarked sardonically, 'Don't tell me—on top of everything else, you're one of those people who're just walking zombies until midday?'

'Not at all,' Michelle answered none too politely. 'I just didn't get much sleep last night, that's all.'

'You'll soon get used to the movement of the boat,' he assured her. 'Then, when you get back on land, you'll find that you won't be able to sleep because everything is so still.'

Michelle pursed her lips into a moue of disbelief, convinced that she wouldn't get a decent night's sleep until they reached Bermuda.

'How about breakfast?' he reminded her. 'I want to get back to the wheel.'

With a feeling of smug triumph, she spooned two eggs out of the pan of boiling water, placed them carefully in eggcups and carried them across to him. Guy looked at them for a moment, up to her waiting expectantly in front of him for a word of praise, then back at the eggs. Slowly he lifted up his spoon and tapped it experimentally against the egg. It made an odd, dull sort of sound. His face quite expressionless, he put down the spoon, picked up one of the eggs and lifted it high above the table, then, as Michelle watched in open-mouthed amazement, he let it drop. The egg hit the wooden table with a loud thud—and bounced!

There was a shattering silence until Guy remarked, almost conversationally, 'I was right, you can't even boil an egg.' Then, 'Have you got something against me, Mitch?'

'N—no.'

'Then why are you trying to either poison me or starve me to death?'

'I'm not! I've never had to boil an egg before. It's not my fault if they came out hard. The gas must have cooked them too quickly.'

Guy stood up and came over to the cooker. 'A poor workman always blames his tools,' he quoted, the contemptuous curl back on his lips. He bent to a cupboard and said, 'Look, this is your first cookery lesson, and I'm going to show you this just once, so you'd better make sure you get it right. This,' he said, thrusting it under her nose, 'is a frying-pan. It is a non-stick frying-pan, so you don't need any fat or cooking oil. You place it on a medium gas and you break the eggs into it. So.' Deftly, he cracked two eggs against the side of the pan and twisted open the shells with one hand, so that the yolks lay round, golden and unbroken. Then he added bacon, mushrooms and tomatoes until the pan was full.

'Where's the bread?' he demanded.

'There isn't any—you wolfed what was left of it last night,' Michelle reminded him nastily.

'Then you'll have to bake some,' he told her, quite unperturbed by her tone.

'Bake some? But I don't know how to.'

'Well, now's your chance to learn.' He crossed to the freezer cabinet and took out two oblong packets. 'Uncooked loaves,' he told her briefly. 'All you have to do is put them in the oven at the required temperature for the required length of time. A child—or should I say, even you—could do it.'

Taking a large plate from the cupboard, he piled everything from the frying pan on to it. 'This is my normal sized breakfast,' he informed her. 'I want this, or its equivalent, waiting for me on the table every morning by seven o'clock. Got that?'

Michelle nodded, but then it occurred to her to ask, 'Where's mine?'

Guy grinned. 'Now that I've shown you how to do it you'll be able to cook your own. It will be good practice for you before tomorrow morning.'

She stared at him speechlessly for a moment, then flounced out of the galley, slamming the door behind her. Let that—that pig eat by himself, she certainly wasn't going to stand there and try to cook with him watching her and probably grinning all over his ugly face at her mistakes.

It was the start of a hellish day that went from bad to worse. Guy's voice over the intercom seemed to be hounding her every five minutes, added to which she threw all the rubbish over the wrong side of the boat so that the wind blew it all back again, she forgot to turn off a tap in the bathroom so that a lot of fresh water was wasted, and she burnt three lots of dough before shem anaged to get two loaves that looked reasonably edible. By the time Guy came down before the evening meal Michelle felt more tired than she'd ever done in her life, her head ached unbearably, and her nerves were stretched to screaming point.

This evening she had put a frozen casserole in the oven, together with an apple pie for dessert, and had vegetables and soup cooking on the hob. Surely tonight he wouldn't be able to find any fault.

But Guy took one mouthful of the soup and then threw his spoon down in disgust. 'What the hell's this? It's stone cold!'

'But it can't be. It's been cooking for ten minutes.'

'Taste it for yourself,' he ordered grimly, and watched as Michelle tasted her own, her face falling in dismay as she realised he was right.

'But I don't understand.'

Guy got up and stepped to the cooker. 'All the pans are nearly cold, and the oven's not much warmer. Don't tell me you forgot to turn the gas on? Even you couldn't be that stupid.'

'Of course I turned it on,' Michelle retorted indignantly.

Picking up a pan, Guy exclaimed, 'The pilot light's gone out. You've used up all the gas. How could you possibly have used up a whole gas cylinder in two days? You'd have had to have the cooker on for the whole day to use that much.'

Michelle had been about to make a rude reply, but came to an abrupt halt as she realised that she had had the cooker on virtually the whole day, trying to bake the rotten bread.

Guilt and consternation must have shown in her face because Guy immediately rounded on her. 'My

God, now I've seen everything! Not only can you not boil an egg but you don't even know when the heat's on underneath a pan. Tell me, Mitch, just what the hell are you good for?' he added, his tone sneering and contemptuous.

'How dare you speak to me like that?' Michelle shouted back at him angrily, the last threads of her temper snapping like fireworks. 'I'm not your servant. All day long you've been ordering me about or calling me over that rotten intercom thing. And I'm sick of it, d'you hear me? I'm just sick of it! Do this, do that. Bring me one thing, clean up something else.' Guy opened his mouth to speak, but she swept on explosively. 'I've had it! I'm not going to lift another finger until we get to Bermuda. I just wish to hell I'd never decided to come on your lousy boat!'

She went to go on, but this time Guy interrupted her angrily. 'You lazy little devil! Just because a few things go wrong you want to run away and hide like a child instead of trying to learn by your mistakes.'

'A few things! You've been picking on me every minute since I came aboard. How was I supposed to know the gas would run out? And it isn't my fault I don't know how to cook.'

Guy's left eyebrow rose interrogatively. 'In that case why did you lie and say that you could when I first talked to you?' he asked in heavy sarcasm.

Deeming it better to ignore that question, Michelle drew herself up to her full height and said tartly, 'Well, you needn't think that I'm going to work for you any more, because I'm not. In future you can do your own cooking and . . .'

'Well, at least I won't get poisoned,' he put in sarcastically.

'And I'll do mine,' Michelle swept on, infuriated

by his interruption. 'And the less I see of you between here and Bermuda, the better I'll like it!'

She went to stalk past him with her chin in the
air, but he reached out and caught her arm, swinging
her round to face him again. 'Oh, no you don't. I'm
not through talking to you yet. I told you when you
came aboard that I'm not carrying any passengers
on this trip. If you want to get to America then
you're going to work whether you like it or not.'

'Oh, no, I'm not! You can't force me.'

The pressure on her arm didn't increase any, but
there was something in his eyes and his voice as he
said softly, 'Oh, yes, I can,' that made Michelle's
face suddenly pale.

Rather unsteadily she said, 'Don't worry, you
won't be out of pocket. I'll pay you for my passage
as soon as I get to Bermuda.'

'But you haven't any money, remember?'

'I'll get some.'

His eyes, cold and contemptuous, looked into hers
as he said with insolence, 'Of course, I'm sure you'd
have no difficulty in doing just that. But even so, the
answer's still no. If I accepted your terms you'd
expect me to feed you and run around for you all
day, as well as sail the boat. You'll work, young
lady, even though you think you're too good for that
kind of thing.'

'I've already told you,' Michelle yelled back at
him, vainly trying to wrench her arm from his grasp.
'I'm not going to do any more of your filthy, horrible
jobs. You can do your own work!'

'All right, if that's the way you want it. Then
there's only one thing left to say.'

Michelle glared at him, hating him. 'And what's
that?'

'If you won't work your passage as crew then

you'll have to work it the other way.'

Michelle's brows drew together in a puzzled frown. 'I don't understand what you mean.'

'Don't you? I think you do. There has to be something you're good at. Maybe it's this.' Taking hold of her other arm, he firmly pulled her towards him and bent to kiss her.

CHAPTER FOUR

For a few minutes Michelle was too startled to react. It was only when she felt the hardness of his lips exploring hers, his hands move from her arms and hold her closer against his lean, muscular body, that she jerked back to life and tried to move away. But his arms held her prisoner, depriving her of movement, and her sound of protest was lost beneath the increasing demands of his mouth as he sought to make her respond. Michelle had been kissed by Peter and other boy-friends often, but none of them had ever had Guy's strength, not only of body, but of mind; it was as if he sought to impose his will on her, to dominate her completely. Vainly she tried to push herself away, but his hand came up and twined in her hair, keeping her still.

It was then that she felt the first stirrings of sexuality deep inside her. They spread like fingers of fire throughout her body until every nerve end was aflame. Slowly her mouth parted beneath his, warm, yielding, and his hands tightened as his kiss became deeper.

When at last he let her go, Michelle took a long, shuddering breath and slowly opened her eyes. Guy was staring down at her, a strange, intent look in his eyes. Huskily he said, 'So now I know what you're good at, don't I? Your cabin or mine?'

'W-what?' Still bemused, her head in a whirl, Michelle hardly took in what he was saying.

'I said your cabin or mine?'

Her eyes flew open. 'You—you mean you want

me to go to bed with you?' she stammered, taking a step away from him.

'That's the general idea,' he agreed calmly.

'But—but I can't!'

'Why not?'

Michelle stared at him, completely disconcerted by his calmness. In her experience, pleas for her to go to bed were usually given during hot, passionate embraces, her boy-friends so roused up that they were almost begging. And she enjoyed the power she had over them, the power to increase their misery by teasing them along a little and then saying no. But never before had any man shown so little reaction after a kiss or asked for—no, demanded—her body so coldbloodedly.

'Because I don't want to, that's why,' she shot back at him angrily.

'Yes, you do. The way you responded when I kissed you proved that beyond any doubt.'

'That—that isn't true.' She tried to say it firmly, but the uncertainty sounded even to her own ears. 'You took me by surprise, that's all.'

'Really?' His left eyebrow rose derisively. 'Well, you won't be taken by surprise this time, will you?'

'No! Don't!' But Michelle's protests were lost under his mouth as he pulled her to him again, more roughly this time, holding her arms imprisoned against his chest so that she was unable to break free. She tried to hold herself rigid, to deny him any response, but within seconds she felt the fire start to spread again and she trembled as his lips, warm and insinuating, forced hers apart. Sense and reason dissolved beneath the wonderful sensations he was arousing in her, she was lost to everything but the awareness of her own need to respond, to go on being held close against him. It was only when she felt his hand come up to caress her breast that some small degree of sanity returned and she pulled away, her breathing ragged and uneven, lips parted, her eyes suddenly frightened.

For a long moment they stared at each other, then Guy said curtly, 'Well?'

Vainly she sought for reasons, time. 'I—I don't know you.'

'That can soon be remedied,' he replied in harsh amusement.

Michelle flushed and there was a note of anger in her tone as she said, 'If you think a couple of kisses are enough to make me want to go to bed with you, then . . .'

'Oh, you want more? By all means, but I assure you that I can demonstrate far better in bed.' Guy stepped purposefully towards her and Michelle moved hastily away until brought up short by the door to the forward cabin.

'No! That isn't what I meant.' Defensively she put up her hands to ward him off.

'Then just what do you mean?' he demanded impatiently.

'Well, I . . . I . . .' She stared at him as he towered over her, a dark stranger whom she hardly knew and who now wanted to make love to her. A man who could disconcertingly rouse her body more quickly and to greater heights than she'd ever known before, but who betrayed absolutely no emotion himself, had uttered no word of endearment or need. 'Why?' The question was asked out of a need for reassurance more than anything else.

'Why?' His eyebrows flew up incredulously, then his mouth twisted into a derisive sneer. 'Let's just say that as we can't live on your cooking we might as well try living on love.'

Michelle's face paled at his tone. 'That isn't funny!' she snapped out.

'No, you're right, it isn't. Why the hell d'you think? You're a woman. You're available and I want you. That's all there is to it.'

She stared at him, open-mouthed, more humiliated than she had ever felt in her life. Then two bright, angry spots of colour appeared in her cheeks and she drew herself up to face him defiantly. 'Well, that's just where you're wrong,' she spat at him. 'I'm not *available* to you now or at any time. You arrogant pig! If you think I even want you to—to touch me, then you're crazy! You're just a . . .'

Her voice was suddenly silenced as Guy's hand shot out and gripped her shoulder. There was a grim, hard look in his dark eyes and for a moment she knew fear, real mind-bending fear as she realised his power and strength, that he only had to exert his will to make her do what he wanted. But then he said coldly, 'All right, I've got the message.' He let go of her and stepped back.

Hastily Michelle lowered her eyes, trying to hide the fear from him, but he must have been aware of it because he said scathingly, 'You crazy little fool.' Then, in a different tone, 'Are you going to work as crew or not?'

'No.' Stubbornly she shook her head.

'Okay, if that's the way you want it. But if you refuse to work your passage—either way—then you don't get a share of the food.'

Michelle looked at him in growing apprehension. 'What do you mean?' Surely he couldn't be that inhuman?

But it seemed he could. 'Quite simply this: if you don't work, you don't eat.'

For a long moment his cool grey eyes challenged

her angry hazel ones, then she snapped, 'Right, that suits me fine.' She went to walk past him, but he deliberately stood in her way for a few seconds longer as he let her see the look of contemptuous disbelief on his face, then he nonchalantly moved to one side and she was able to sweep past and leave him alone with his cold, uncooked meal.

Back in her cabin, Michelle flung herself down on the bunk, seething with anger. The arrogant, conceited swine! How dared he treat her like some cheap bed-hopping tart? Work her passage, indeed! God, she'd hardly stopped working from the minute he'd first found her on his rotten boat! She glared malevolently in the direction of the galley where she could hear him moving about, her thoughts vicious. Just who the hell did he think he was anyway? Why, he must be at least ten years older than she was, if not more. He was nothing but a dirty old man! The fact that she'd told him she was twenty-four she dismissed as irrelevant; he was still virtually a cradle-snatcher. He was more her parents' generation than hers, in fact her mother had had several lovers who were about Guy's age, if not younger, and . . .

Her thoughts came to an abrupt halt as a mental picture of Guy with her mother filled her mind. Was he the type that the beautiful Adele Verlaine would go for, would invite into the perfumed sanctum of her mirrored boudoir and into the silk-sheeted softness of her huge four-poster bed?

Somehow the thought grated and Michelle pushed it resolutely away, cursing the bad luck that had made the tide carry her to this boat of all the boats that must have been moored in the Thames estuary that night. Anybody else would have realised straight away that she wasn't used to having to work and would have been kind to her. But not Guy

Farringdon. Oh no, he had to either treat her like an unpaid servant, or demand that she share his bed—bunk. Well, he needn't think that he was going to intimidate her by his ultimatum! She'd rather starve to death than have him lay even a finger on her again.

She turned over and gazed unseeingly out of the window at the darkening sky, trying to keep her thoughts from remembering the way she'd felt when he'd kissed her, but it was no good, they kept straying back, and in the end she gave up trying, just let her mind wander where it would. Did all older men kiss like that? she wondered. With such complete domination and expertise. Did the youths, whose wet, full-mouthed, breathless embraces that she fought off now, eventually turn into men like Guy whose hard-lipped kisses could arouse emotions inside her she'd never known existed? Somehow she doubted it; she could never imagine Guy as being the fumbling type at all, he was the sort of person who would become expert in everything he did, whether it was sailing a boat or making love to a woman.

Michelle shivered and wished suddenly, fervently, that she had never embarked on this crazy adventure, and that she'd asked him to take her back to England when she had the opportunity. It was too late now, of course; even if she told him the truth he wouldn't turn back. Just the few days that she had known him had taught her that he was too implacable to do anything he didn't want to: and he most certainly wouldn't want to lose the chance of getting orders for some of his precious boats. So she would just have to put up with him for the rest of the voyage. She tried to work out how much longer it would take, but she hadn't the faintest idea where Bermuda was. Presumably it was somewhere near

the coast of America as they had to go to it on the
way, and she had a vague idea that it took five days
to sail from Southampton to New York, so, as they
had been travelling for near enough three days, they
would reach Bermuda either tomorrow or the day
after. So it would be quicker to go on than to turn
back anyway. What did they call it on aeroplanes—
the point of no return?

For a while she dwelt in her imagination on the
scene when she told the authorities in Bermuda who
she was and they sent for her parents. And what a
shock it would be for that louse, Guy Farringdon, as
well! Michelle thought lovingly of the humiliation
he would feel when he realised how she had tricked
him. Then he'd be sorry for propositioning her,
making her work so hard and go without food. She
hadn't thought too much about that aspect of their
quarrel yet; she could last out till tomorrow, of
course, but if they didn't reach Bermuda until the
day after...Resolutely she turned her thoughts away
from food and tried to think about what she would
say to her parents, but her mind kept swinging
angrily back to her fight with Guy. If he thought she
was going to give in he was mistaken; no way was
she going to submit to his despotic manner or his
sexual demands. Just because he was used to giving
orders and everyone jumped to obey it didn't mean
that he could bully her. And was he used to having
women fall into his arms whenever he made a pass?
Uneasily Michelle sat up, clasped her arms round
her knees and rested her chin on them. She supposed
there were some women who liked the autocratic
type, who were content to be dominated. Not that
she was, of course, she was a child of her times who
believed that women were at least equal, if not supe-
rior, to the male sex. And that there were, she was

willing to concede, some women who might even think Guy was attractive in a hard, lean-featured kind of way, although personally she thought him much too tough-looking to be handsome. But, all in all, she had no doubt that he had no difficulty in attracting women, especially any woman that he really wanted.

Her thoughts wandered then until the piquant aroma of hot food reached her nostrils and made her realise how hungry she was. The beast—he must have finished cooking the casserole. Damn the man! She'd show him that she wasn't to be browbeaten even if she did go hungry!

She lasted that night and all the next day, a day of increasing boredom in which she catnapped on her bunk and gazed out of the window and tried to ignore the protest noises her stomach was making. Every minute she expected land to appear on the horizon, but they travelled on over an empty sea without any sign of another ship or even a seabird to break the monotony. Several times she heard Guy in the galley and at breakfast and dinnertime the savoury aroma of cooking food reached into her cabin and made her drool. Never before had she ever had to miss a meal, and she was amazed at how quickly she felt hungry.

In the evening she heard Guy whistling in the bathroom as he prepared for bed, evidently quite impervious to the misery he was causing her. She lay in her bunk in the darkness, having showered and washed her underclothes earlier to try to take her mind off the fact that he was tucking into another huge meal. The pig! The rotten swine! Angrily she punched her pillow and turned restlessly on the bunk. Guy walked past her cabin on the way to his own and she heard him moving around in there for a while and the bunk creak as he heaved his big frame into it, then all was still and quiet except for the usual sounds of the sea and the boat, sounds that she was becoming more used to now and which didn't frighten her so much.

For what seemed like hours she lay there, unable to sleep, the pangs of hunger clawing at her stomach, thinking of all the lovely food that was just sitting out there, a few feet away, in the galley. Suddenly Michelle could bear it no longer; she thrust aside the sleeping bag and, in the rays of moonlight coming through the window, found Guy's bathrobe and pulled it on to cover her nakedness. Then, walking on tiptoe even though her feet were bare, she crept over to the door, gently eased back the bolt and slowly opened it, praying that it wouldn't creak. Hardly daring to breathe, she padded silently down the corridor to the galley and let herself in, carefully shutting the door behind her before she turned on the light.

Once inside Michelle worked fast, cutting herself a thick ham sandwich and a chunk of yesterday's apple pie, then took a whole packet of cracker biscuits, butter and a large wedge of cheese from the fridge. She was going to need enough to last her for breakfast tomorrow too. She piled everything into a small box and a bottle of lemonade to wash it down with went under her arm, then she turned out the light and slowly opened the door. All was quiet, there were no sounds other than natural ones. With a sigh of relief, Michelle carried her booty down the corridor, almost wishing that Guy snored. It would be worth having to listen to the noise through the bulkhead during the night, to know that he was safely asleep now. Because her hands were full she had to shoulder her cabin door open and put the box and

bottle on the floor while she quickly turned, shut the
door and bolted it. Safe! With a little gleeful laugh
of delight and triumph she turned on the light,
reaching ravenously for the food.

'A midnight feast?'

Guy's sarcastic voice made her head jerk up and
then freeze in stunned disbelief as she saw him leaning negligently against her bunk, bare-chested,
wearing just a pair of jeans.

Straightening up, he went on, 'I knew you'd
try this some time tonight. It's just the kind of sneaky
trick you'd pull.' Two paces took him across the
cabin to her side so that he could see into the box.
'As I said, quite a feast you've got there.' Slowly he
lifted his head and looked at her, his eyes menacing.
'Now take it back.'

Michelle found that she was held prisoner by his
eyes, unable to look away even though she tried.
Her heart had begun to pound and she instinctively
took a step backwards.

'I I thought you were asleep,' she stammered
lamely.

His tone was dry as he replied, 'That's obvious.'
He looked at her expectantly, and when she didn't
move, added curtly, 'You heard me, take it back.'

'No.'

The denial just came out, without any conscious
decision on Michelle's part, and disconcerted her far
more than it did Guy.

His eyes narrowed and he took a step towards her.
'Are you trying to defy me?'

Too late, she tried to play on his sympathy. 'I'm
hungry.'

'It's your own fault. You know the terms.'

Somehow she dragged her eyes away from his, but
then found that she was looking at the broad expanse

of his smooth, tanned chest and lean, hard stomach and hastily raised her eyes again. Strange things were happening inside her and she felt curiously breathless and confused. To cover it she took refuge in anger.

'You have no right to dictate to me. I offered to pay my fare.'

'But not in any form that was acceptable to me. I don't want your money, I just want your services— one way or another.' His eyes travelled down her in insolent appraisal as he spoke, and, glancing down, Michelle saw that the bathrobe had loosened, opening almost down to her waist. Hastily she went to re-tie it, but Guy moved the box of food out of the way with his foot and said, 'Why bother?' and backed her against the door.

Michelle stared up at him, her eyes wide and scared, but completely fascinated, unable to move. She knew what was going to happen, but her throat felt so constricted that she couldn't speak, and all the strength seemed to have drained from her body, so that she could only lean against the door and wait as he deliberately reached out and put a finger behind the belt of the robe, slowly drew the ends apart until they opened and dropped to hang at her sides. The robe was too voluminous to reveal her body completely, but it opened enough to show him the enticing shadows of the curve of her breasts, and the gleam of light on one long, slim thigh.

Guy's eyes wandered down, unhurried, taking his time, while Michelle stood as though turned to stone, waiting, just waiting. He didn't say anything, just parted the robe a little more and put his hands inside to cup her breasts. A shudder of ecstasy and delight ran through her as she felt the firmness of his touch. She moaned and shut her eyes, her mouth parting sensuously. She knew that it was dangerous, that she ought to stop him, but she *wanted* him to touch her, wanted him to go on caressing, fondling, sending these waves of desire through her body. His fingers tightened as he felt her tremble, squeezed so that her breasts hardened and she let out a moaning gasp of pleasure. She moved voluptuously, finding his caresses so exciting that she could hardly bear it. Her skin felt as if it was on fire. Tiny beads of perspiration formed on her brow and on her upper lip. Slowly she opened her eyes, heavy-lidded with desire, her breath ragged, sighing.

He wasn't looking directly at her. His eyes were intent on what he was doing as his hands expertly fondled and played with her breasts. But then the sound of her breathing must have changed, or perhaps he felt her looking at him, because he looked up and their eyes met and held. There was no passion in his face; desire, yes, but that was physical, not emotional. And there was no pleasure; in fact his face looked almost stern, his lips drawn into a thin line, his jaw hard and determined. It was as if he had coldbloodedly set out to rouse her sensuality so that she would give herself to him willingly, but all his emotions were held under an iron control, giving nothing of himself in return, just taking her to satisfy his physical needs. It was almost as if he didn't really want to touch her, was only doing it because she had refused him the first time and he needed to inflame her senses to fever pitch to make her unable to resist him.

Michelle stiffened, but he immediately sensed the change in her and moved his hands down to her waist and then low on to her hips. Then he slowly, deliberately pulled her against him so that her burning flesh touched the smooth, cool skin of his chest. Involuntarily she cried out, closing her eyes again and putting her hands up to his shoulders, her nails digging into his hard muscles as he moved against her. 'Guy! Oh, Guy.' She gasped out his name, lost again in rapture, and lifted her head, her mouth parting for his kiss.

Opening her eyes for a brief instant, she had a fleeting glimpse of his face as he bent to place his mouth on hers and in that second she saw and recognised the calculating triumph in his grey eyes, the slightly contemptuous curl of his lips.

Immediately she jerked her head away, her eyes wide with shock as she stared into his face, seeking there something that would give the lie to her fears, but finding only corroboration in his frown of annoyance. Using all her strength, she wrenched herself free from his hold and hastily pulled the robe close round herself again, crossing her arms over her chest in a protective gesture. She felt as if she had been used, defiled.

'Leave me alone!'

The frown deepened and an exasperated look came into his eyes. 'Now what?'

'You heard me. Keep away from me. I don't want you to touch me.'

Guy laughed shortly, unpleasantly. 'Oh, yes, you do.'

He reached for her again, but Michelle shrank back against the door. 'I mean it.'

The exasperation changed to anger. 'For God's sake stop playing games. You want to have sex as much as I do. No woman responds like you did unless she's turned on.'

The bluntness of his tone shocked her almost as much as the crudity of his words. 'How *dare* you speak to me like that? Just because we're by ourselves on this boat you think you can force yourself on me . . .'

'Oh, no,' he interrupted brusquely. 'I've never forced myself on an unwilling female yet and I certainly don't intend to start with you. Not that I have to,' he added with a sneer, 'because even though you try to deny it, you're not only willing but eager.'

Michelle's face flamed, knowing it was true, but she still denied it. 'No, I don't want you to make love to me.'

His lip curled. 'Love doesn't come into it.'

'That's perfectly obvious,' Michelle agreed bitterly. 'It's nothing but sex with you. You don't even care about my feel . . .'

'Good Lord, is that what this is all about?' he demanded disparagingly. 'Are you the type who has to be flattered and complimented and told that a man's in love with you before you'll go to bed with him?'

She stared at him, realising that that was exactly what she wanted, but also knowing that even if he did say it he wouldn't mean a word of it. He was so cold, so unmoved. Nothing in her experience had ever prepared her for someone like him, and she felt completely out of her depth. The physical desire he had aroused in her had been devastating, almost overwhelming, and it would be so easy to say, yes, that's what I want, and to lose herself again in his embrace as he said the words that made it all right, that made her forget that to him she was only a convenient body in whom he could satisfy his needs. Forget for the brief time in which it was happening, maybe, but remember with regret and bitterness for the rest of her life.

'Well?' he demanded impatiently. 'I'm quite willing to provide some romance, if that's what you need.'

'That won't be necessary.' Slowly Michelle straightened up from the door. She still felt shaken and nervous but managed to say, 'All right, you win. I'll work as crew again.'

His eyes narrowed. 'Maybe the choice isn't open any more.'

For a moment panic filled her, but then she faced up to him. 'You said you wouldn't force yourself on me.'

He had taken a step towards her, but stopped abruptly at that. His jaw thrust forward as he said harshly, 'I don't like playing games, Mitch, and I especially don't like little girls who play hard to get.'

'I'm not—playing games.'

'Then why not take the easy way out?'

She didn't understand for a minute, then realised that he considered going to bed with him would be an easier option than working. Balefully she answered, 'I *am* taking the easier way out.'

Guy frowned and for a moment they glared at each other. Michelle wished he would just go away and leave her alone, but he seemed unwilling to end it. 'Just what the hell is it you want from me?'

'Nothing. I didn't ask you to start kissing me or— or touching me. And you needn't think I liked it, because I didn't.'

He laughed sneeringly. 'Oh, you liked it all right, let's not be in any doubt about that. And you knew darn well what to expect from the moment you said you wanted to stay on board and not be put ashore.'

'No, I didn't. I just wanted a passage out to America, that's all.'

Guy snorted derisively. 'Don't try to con me! You came into this with your eyes open. As soon as you realised that we were alone you knew that I'd make a pass and expect you to reciprocate.'

'No. No, I didn't,' Michelle shook her head urgently. 'I just wanted to—to get away for a while, and this seemed an ideal opportunity. I thought it would be a—sort of adventure.'

His eyebrows rose in disbelief. 'Don't give me that innocent little girl act! You've probably been to bed with a dozen men, besides the one you went to France with.'

Michelle's face paled, only now realising in what danger her fertile imagination had placed her, yet it had all seemed so innocent and easy at the time. No way had she expected Guy to take her for easy game, the sort of girl who would be willing to pay for her passage by going to bed with him. It had just never occurred to her. She had been so intent on teaching her parents a lesson that she hadn't even thought of any danger to herself. If Guy had been different, had been the type of man who undressed you with his eyes and made lewd comments, she would never even have contemplated staying on board, but he hadn't seemed like that at all and it hadn't crossed her mind that she couldn't trust him. But perhaps instinct had been right and if he knew the truth about her he'd leave her alone. After all, he had stopped when she'd said no. Michelle looked up at him uncertainly, not wanting to tell him who she was but aware that she couldn't go on letting him believe the worst of her.

Eventually she said reluctantly, 'I—I'm afraid I lied to you about that.'

Guy's eyes narrowed. 'Go on.'

'I was at a party at a night club by the river and—well, we'd had quite a lot to drink and someone dared me to swim out to your boat. So I did.'

'Which river?'

'The Thames.'

'Good God! Do you mean to say that you were aboard all the time I was going across the Channel to France?'

'Yes, I suppose so. I don't really remember. I was feeling rather tired, you see, and I fell asleep.'

'Probably dead drunk, more likely,' Guy stated sardonically. 'You were lucky you didn't drown.' He looked at her speculatively. 'But why didn't you tell me all this at first? Why spin me that story about having been to France for the weekend with a boyfriend?'

Michelle shrugged rather helplessly. 'It—er—seemed a good idea at the time,' she answered lamely.

He looked at her sharply. 'You wouldn't have lied about your age too, by any chance?'

Cornered, she could only nod reluctantly.

'So just how old are you?'

'Er—nineteen.'

He stared at her, appalled, then said vehemently, '*You* are not fit to be let out alone. Of all the stupid, insane . . .' A thought occurred to him. 'You say you were dared to swim out to the boat—did anyone see you board it?'

Michelle saw immediately what danger lay in a truthful answer to that one, so crossed her fingers and answered airily, 'Oh, yes, a whole crowd of people. But when I got on board I realised it was empty and there was no dinghy to row back in, and I didn't think I'd have enough strength to swim.'

'I see.' Guy was still looking at her suspiciously and she tried to make her face as innocent as possible, but his next question really threw her. 'Do your parents know where you are?' he demanded bluntly.

A bleak look came into her eyes as she answered

stiltedly, 'My parents were divorced a long time ago. They don't care about me.'

Guy looked at her searchingly. 'Is that the truth?'

'Oh, yes.' She laughed mirthlessly. 'That's definitely the truth.'

He gazed at her for a long moment, a surprised, slightly troubled look in his grey eyes at her reply. 'Are you sure that there's no one who ought to be told?'

Her chin came up. 'No, no one,' she said decisively.

Guy turned away, took a couple of paces across the cabin, then saw the box of food on the floor. He swung back to her, anger again in his face. 'You young fool! Why the hell didn't you tell me the truth from the start?'

'I didn't think you'd take me with you if I did.'

'You're damn right I wouldn't. And I would never have . . .' he checked abruptly.

'Tried to have sex with me,' Michelle supplied for him, feeling suddenly safe and confident again. 'Why don't you say it? You were ready enough to use the word before.'

'Maybe I was. But you don't have to worry, I won't try it again.'

Which should have been an extremely comforting assurance but which somehow left her with very mixed feelings and nothing to say.

Guy stooped and picked up the box of food. 'You might as well eat this in the galley.'

Michelle followed him out of the cabin and willingly sat down at the table and began to devour a ham sandwich hungrily. It tasted delicious, better than any she'd ever eaten before. Guy made a couple of mugs of coffee, put one on the table in front of her, then sat down opposite, watching her broodingly. Her first cravings satisfied, Michelle glanced up and caught him watching her.

'Thanks for the coffee.'

He nodded absently, then said abruptly, 'Yesterday you offered to pay me for your passage. Just how did you expect to get the money when you landed in Bermuda?'

'My parents are quite well off; they make me an allowance. I would have arranged for some money to be sent through a bank,' she told him, then thought that once she made known her identity to the authorities in Bermuda she'd have no difficulty in obtaining money for clothes and things straightaway. 'Why, how did you think I was going to pay you?'

Guy shrugged, his lips curling. 'There are plenty of opportunities for the kind of girl I thought you were to earn money in whatever country she happens to end up in.'

'Oh!' She flushed. 'I suppose you've,' she sought for a word, then said, 'had sex with a lot of women like that?'

His brows drew together into a frown. 'That's none of your damn business,' he told her acidly.

'It is when you nearly added me to the list,' Michelle retorted.

'Only because you left yourself wide open to it. But I was beginning to realise you weren't what you claimed anyway.'

'Oh. How?'

A sardonic look came into the grey eyes as he said bluntly, 'You're extremely inexperienced.'

'Oh,' Michelle said again, blushing furiously and looking down at her half-eaten sandwich, feeling suddenly as if she was back at school and being told off for not working hard enough.

Guy picked up his empty mug and took it across to the sink to rinse it out. Afterwards he turned and said, 'I meant what I said about not taking any passengers; I shall expect you to do your share of the work.'

Michelle looked up at him. He was so tall that his head almost brushed the ceiling of the cabin and there were hard, thick muscles in his arms and shoulders. The skin on his smooth, hairless chest still had the faded tan of last summer and he looked very fit and strong, not an ounce of superfluous flesh round his waist or on the smooth, flat plane of his stomach above the top of the jeans. Her throat felt suddenly tight and she quickly lowered her head again. Her voice unsteady, she answered, 'I—I know. It's all right, I want to.' She smiled uncertainly. 'After all, we'll be in Bermuda tomorrow, so you'll only have to survive my cooking until then.'

His eyebrows rose. 'What makes you think that?'

'Well,' she looked at him in perplexity, 'it takes five days to get from Southampton to New York, so it can't take that much longer to get to Bermuda. And we've been at sea nearly as long as that already.'

'What do you think this boat is—the *Queen Elizabeth*? We're making a good rate of knots, but even at this speed it will take us about another five days or so before we reach Hamilton.'

'Five days!' Michelle stared at him in horror. He had known that when he'd denied her any food. Heavens, she could have starved to death in that time!

Something of what she was thinking must have shown in her face, because Guy laughed in genuine amusement. 'Is that how you managed to last out so long—because you thought we'd be putting into port shortly? I expected you to capitulate before this.'

His words made them both remember just how he had expected her to capitulate. Michelle looked down at her plate and concentrated on eating the last bite of her sandwich. Guy was silent until she'd finished, then said tersely, 'If you've had enough you'd better go and get some sleep. It's almost two in the morning. And I too,' he added wryly, 'could do with some rest.'

Michelle stood up at once. 'Yes, of course. I'm sorry.' She paused awkwardly. 'I'm sorry about lying to you, too.'

He nodded, and after a minute she turned to leave, but at the door he called her name. 'Mitch.'

'Yes?' She stopped with her hand on the door knob, half turned away from him.

He paused for a long moment, his eyes studying her face, then said abruptly, 'Are you still a virgin?'

No man, or woman either come to that, had ever dared to ask her such a personal question. She should have been angry or indignant, at the least embarrassed, but strangely she felt none of those emotions. It was merely a direct question that required a direct answer, and she somehow knew that it was important that she tell him the truth and not try to prevaricate. So she simply said, 'Yes, I am.'

He didn't answer and she didn't expect him to. He merely nodded and she went on her way to her cabin.

CHAPTER FIVE

LIGHT penetrating the curtains woke Michelle the next morning and she lay lazily in the bunk for a few minutes, her mind immediately full of the show-down with Guy the night before. On the whole, she thought she had come out of it quite well; she had had to tell him some of the truth, but not enough to put paid to the game she was playing. Then she remembered that she had agreed to work and her mouth pouted into a moue of distaste, but she had been so bored alone in her cabin when she'd been 'on strike' that the prospect wasn't as displeasing as it had been before. Kneeling up, she pulled back the curtains and the cabin was instantly filled with sun-light, the heat of which she could feel through the glass of the window. She had no means of telling the time, but from the position of the sun she could guess that Guy would soon be yelling for his breakfast. She'd better get to work.

Maybe it was because she wasn't hungry any more, maybe the change in the weather, or perhaps it was just because she now felt more at ease that Michelle began to hum a catchy pop tune as she cooked Guy's breakfast, carefully cracking the eggs so that the yolks didn't break when she put them in the frying-pan. It was very warm in the galley and she slid the windows wide open, enjoying the touch of the sun on her bare arms.

'Well, well!' Guy's mocking voice in the doorway made her turn to look at him. 'Can this be the same sulky stowaway I had on board yesterday?'

93

Michelle laughed. 'It's the sun. I'm a summer person, I only blossom when the sun shines.'

'In that case I'm extremely thankful that we've reached a latitude in which we should be in constant sunshine from now on,' he remarked, sitting down at the table.

'Have we really? Lovely! I'll be able to get a tan—when I've finished my work, of course,' she added hastily.

Guy said casually, 'Oh, you'll be able to get brown while you're swabbing the decks.'

Michelle looked at him indignantly, but then saw from his mocking grin that he was teasing her and she laughed again. Anxiously she transferred the food from the frying pan to a plate, praying that she wouldn't break the eggs, then triumphantly placed the plate in front of him, looking at him expectantly.

For a moment he looked down at it contemplatively, then raised his eyes to her apprehensive face and said, 'So I've been proved wrong twice—the age of miracles hasn't passed. It looks perfect.'

'You'd better taste it first,' she warned him, but turned away to cook something for herself, well pleased. At least he was as unstinting with his praise as he had previously been with his condemnation. But she did wonder what the first miracle had been.

After breakfast Guy went up to the flying-bridge leaving Michelle to clean up the galley, bathroom and cabins, but as the sun rose she became increasingly hot in the bunched-up jeans. She contemplated cutting the legs down to turn them into shorts, which would help to make her legs feel cooler, but would do nothing to relieve the prickly heat round her waistline where she had, of necessity, to pull the belt tight to keep them up at all. And besides, Guy might have something to say about her cutting his jeans up. She soldiered on for a while, then, unable to stand it any longer, simply took the jeans off completely. The relief was exquisite; she felt as if she'd been in a sauna and had walked out into the cold air. When her skin had cooled down she went into her cabin and stood on tiptoe so that she could see her bottom half in the built-in mirror. Actually Guy's tee-shirt was so long on her that it fitted her like a mini-dress and completely covered her pants. Picking up the belt, she slipped it round her waist and experimentally tightened it. The soft blue material of the tee-shirt clung to the fullness of her uptilted breasts and the curves of her hips, the belt accentuating the slimness of her waist. Below it her legs stretched long and slender down to her small, delicately-boned feet. She had good legs, she knew, they were one of her best features, but for a moment she contemplated putting the jeans back on again, aware that the figure-hugging garment made her look sexy and worried what Guy's reaction would be. Not that she was afraid he'd make another pass; it wasn't that, because he'd given his word and she knew, instinctively, that she could trust him. No, it was something in herself that told her she ought not to do it. But after a moment she shrugged; it was just too hot to wear the silly old jeans, and she kicked them into a corner—then realised that there was no one to clear up after her and so picked them up, folded them and put them away in a drawer—an action that would have made her mother's maid agree with Guy that miracles could happen.

The sun was drawing her like a magnet, and, as soon as she'd done her chores, Michelle climbed the ladder to the deck. For a few moments she stood at the rail, savouring the sun on her body, feeling it enfold her, turning the light down of hairs on her

arms to a golden blonde. The deck felt hot under
her bare feet as she padded slowly towards the bows,
the wind catching her hair as she moved out of the
shelter of the main cabin. The sea looked completely
different today; before it had seemed like an enemy,
a malevolent element that had tossed the boat and
made her sick the first night and had kept her awake
with its noise on others, a vast, grey, empty expanse
of alien water that could easily pluck their fragile
craft down into its endless depths. But today the sea
was an incredible blue, the waves capped by racing
white horses whose spray broke into a million
crystals, each facet reflecting the brightness of the
sun until it hurt her eyes to look and she had to
shield them from its brilliance. Leaning over the rail,
she could see a shoal of fish darting along beside
them, keeping pace even at the speed they were
travelling, their silvery scales flashing and glinting
for a few seconds as they came near the surface, then
fading as the fish dived down again or were over-
taken by the bubbling white waters of the boat's
wake. The tang of the sea was very strong; she
couldn't remember having ever really smelt it before.
But now it filled her nostrils, clean and salty, carried
on the breeze, an aroma as old as time itself.

'Do you want to try and catch some?'

Guy's voice broke into her reverie and she turned
to look up at him leaning over the rail of the fly-
bridge.

'I don't know how,' she called back, raising her
voice above the breeze and the sound of the sea.

'I'll teach you. Stay there.'

He put the boat on auto-pilot, disappeared below
for a few minutes and then came back carrying a
fishing rod. For the first time he noticed that she
wasn't wearing his jeans. His eyes ran over her and

his brows flickered, but Michelle couldn't tell whether he was angry or not. She found herself saying defensively, 'The jeans were so thick, I was much too hot in them.'

He nodded slightly, but merely said, 'Come on up to the fishing platform in the bow.'

He led her right up to the front of the boat, the bow as he called it, where a narrow railed platform projected over the sea for a couple of feet. Michelle had noticed it before but had had no idea of its purpose. There was a safety belt fitted to the rails and this he clipped round her waist. 'Just in case you catch a whale,' he told her with wry mockery. Then he patiently showed her how to bait the line and how to cast it so she didn't get it caught up in the superstructure behind her. She was clumsy at first, finding the whole thing difficult and almost ready to give up. A week ago she would have done, rather than run the risk of making a fool of herself, but today was different; today she had managed to cook breakfast without ruining it, the sun was shining and she had the feeling that she could do anything if she really tried. So she laughed when the line wound itself round the rail of the flying-bridge and Guy had to climb up and release it for her, and didn't instead get cross with the unwieldy rod.

'No, like this.' He came up behind her and moved her hands on the rod, covering them with his own. 'Put all the movement in your wrists.'

He went through the motions with her a couple of times, but somehow Michelle couldn't concentrate. She could feel the heat from his body close against her own, the powerfulness in his hands and arms as they guided hers so easily, smell the hot, masculine aroma of his skin, slightly beaded with perspiration.

'Now you try it,' he commanded, moving slightly to one side.

Obediently she took hold of the rod again, but her hands were unsteady and she had to look at him. He seemed quite impervious to their closeness, merely concentrating on the job in hand, but then he glanced at her and his eyes narrowed in immediate understanding and warning. Curtly he said, 'Get on with it.'

He stayed beside her until she could handle the rod well enough not to entangle it, then left her to manage by herself. Michelle didn't mind, she found she quite enjoyed standing up here in the bow like a living figurehead as the boat cleaved its way through the sea. It was certainly a pleasant and lazy way to pass the time. Suddenly the line jerked in her hands and she almost dropped it. A fish! She'd actually caught a fish. Excitedly she yelled to Guy and he ran down to help her.

'Take it slowly,' he warned her. 'Play it out. Don't try to hurry it.'

Michelle couldn't have done if she'd tried. The rod felt as if it was being pulled out of her hands and Guy had to help her hold it. She would gladly have relinquished it to him, but he made her keep hold of it, just standing ready in case it got too much for her. At last the fight ended and she was able to reel the fish in and pull it up on to the deck. It was quite a big fish, weighing several pounds, and it lay on the deck at her feet with its mouth open and gills flapping weakly, its beautiful silvery scales already turning to dull grey as it struggled to get back in the water.

'Quickly, throw it back!' Michelle exclaimed as Guy bent to remove the hook from the fish's mouth.

He glanced up at her in surprise. 'Why? This one's big enough. It's a yellowtail snapper.'

The fish thrashed its tail in a last frenzy, desperately trying to escape, but Guy held it firmly as he hit it hard, just once, against the deck, killing it instantly.

'You've killed it!' Michelle stared down at him in horror. 'How could you?'

Guy stood up with the fish in his hands. 'Because we're going to have it for supper, of course. Why the hell do you think we were trying to catch one?'

'I thought it was just for sport, that you'd throw it back. You didn't have to kill it—you've got plenty of food in the freezer.'

'I prefer fresh fish.' Calmly he began to dismantle the rod.

'Then you're just a sadist!' Michelle told him angrily, her voice rising. 'That fish was beautiful and you had no right to kill it.'

'Oh, for God's sake grow up. Do you think a shark would think you were beautiful and leave you alone if you fell in the sea?' he demanded brutally. 'Man has been preying on other animals to survive since time immemorial. It's the law of the jungle, Mitch.'

'I still think you were just being cruel. And if you think I'm going to eat any of that fish, you're crazy!'

His eyes met hers levelly. 'Eat it or not as you like, I couldn't care less. But you're certainly going to clean it and cook it for me.'

'Oh, no, I'm not! You can do your own dirty work.'

She moved to stride away from him, but before she quite realised what was happening Guy reached out and grabbed her wrist, at the same time dropping the fish into her arms. It was wet and slippery against her bare skin and she gave a cry of mingled horror and revulsion, hating the feel of it and the way its dead, empty little eye stared up at her.

'No, take it away. Please!'

She tried to drop it on the deck, but Guy held her arms firmly round the fish, using his strength to make her obey him.

'It's just a fish, Mitch, that's all,' he told her, his voice harsh. 'It's no different from the frozen stuff you buy in the supermarket. Just because that fish comes in a colourful package it doesn't mean that they weren't alive once and swimming freely in the sea. But you don't go into hysterics about eating those, do you? Do you?' he demanded when she didn't answer at once.

Slowly Michelle shook her head. 'No, I suppose not.' She lifted her head and looked at him, her hazel eyes close to tears. 'But this was different somehow. They looked so beautiful swimming along beside the boat with the sun shining on them. They were so alive. And,' she turned her head away, 'and I've never seen anything killed before.'

For a moment he didn't answer and when he did his voice sounded strange, oddly unlike him. 'Well, now you have. And I don't suppose it will be the last by any means. Take it down to the galley and wash it, then leave it until I have time to come down and show you how to gut it.'

He turned away dismissively while he finished putting away the rod, leaving Michelle to gaze at his broad back uncertainly, but he didn't turn round or even look at her. It seemed that, as usual, she had no choice but to obey him, so she slowly turned and carried the fish below, her skin flinching away from its cold sliminess.

For the rest of the day she was subdued and took care to keep out of Guy's way, but made no demur when he came into the galley and showed her how to clean the fish. It made her stomach turn, but somehow she managed to stay and watch. Afterwards, when it didn't look like a fish any more and was in a dish in the oven, Guy put an understanding hand on her shoulder. 'You did fine,' he told her approvingly.

Michelle moved forward and leant her head against his chest, feeling suddenly trembly with relief now that it was all over. 'I was afraid I'd be sick,' she admitted.

'You did okay. I'll make a fisherman out of you yet.'

She smiled a little, glad that he was pleased with her, and relaxed against him.

His hand tightened on her shoulder and she could feel his fingers biting into her flesh, then, abruptly, he moved away. 'Keep your eye on it; don't let it burn,' he instructed curtly. 'I'm going up to the wheelhouse to radio in.'

They ate their meal mostly in silence, Michelle trying to force herself not to think of what she was eating but not being very successful, and Guy of course tucking into his food with his usual appetite. She thought, scathingly, that he had no finer feelings at all, then felt instantly ashamed; a lesser man wouldn't have taken no for an answer, would have just forced himself on her and taken what he wanted. That thought made her hand tremble and she pushed her plate away, unable to even pretend to eat. Sitting back in her seat, she sipped her glass of wine and watched Guy under her lashes. His table manners were excellent and his hands, although strong and tanned, weren't rough or the nails dirty or broken. His fingers were long, sensitive; she remembered the way they'd touched and caressed her breasts and she stirred restlessly in her seat, gripping the stem of the glass hard. Guy glanced across at her and she quickly got up, afraid that he would read her thoughts.

'I'll make some coffee,' she muttered unnecessarily, turning her back on him.

He'd finished eating by the time she'd made it, and lit a cigarette. For a few minutes he contemplated her over the smoke as she stirred her coffee, her head bent so that her hair hid her face. Then he said abruptly, 'How long ago did your parents split up?'

'What? Oh, ages ago.' She shrugged. 'I was only about six when my father left; I can hardly remember them being together.'

'Have they remarried?'

'My father has—a couple of times, but my mother hasn't.' Despite herself she couldn't keep the bitterness out of her voice and Guy looked at her sharply.

'Do you blame your father for that—for marrying someone else?'

Michelle laughed shortly. 'Good heavens, no! Even a saint couldn't live with my mother. None of her lovers last very long.' She deliberately used the word to try and shock him, but he merely asked,

'Why don't they last very long?'

'Because they get tired of having to behave like sycophantic lapdogs, I suppose. Or else she gets tired of them,' Michelle added, picking up a fork and digging it into the tablecloth. 'But then she just goes on to the next lover. Oh, she doesn't have any trouble finding them; they all queue up to have an affair w . . .' she stopped abruptly, 'with her. You see, my mother isn't like me, she's very beautiful.' She laughed mirthlessly again. 'I'm afraid I'm a great disappointment to them.'

Guy's hand came out and covered hers, holding it still, stopping the vicious action of the fork. Roughly he said, 'Stop selling yourself short.' Adding as Michelle's eyes came quickly up to meet his, 'You'll do. Believe me, you'll do.'

The sincerity in his face and his voice threw her, made her feel suddenly shy. He released her hand and sat back again, watching her.

'Why did you ask me about my parents?' she asked, to fill the silence.

'It seemed strange that they wouldn't worry where you were, when you're so young.' He didn't add 'and so innocent', although the words hung in the air.

For a moment Michelle felt ashamed about deceiving him and perversely got annoyed with him for making her feel it. 'What the hell does it matter to you that my parents were incapable of living together?'

His eyes narrowed. 'It seems to mean a lot to you.'

'No, it doesn't, I couldn't care less. I certainly don't need them,' she said loudly, too loudly.

Guy pulled on his cigarette, studying her averted face. Slowly he said, 'Then maybe you blame them for splitting up, for not making more of an effort to stay together for your sake.'

Michelle's head came up, her eyes bleak and vulnerable. 'They don't care about me—they never have. They were both too wrapped up in their own careers, their own lives, to care about me. All they ever did was to yell at each other, and argue . . .' She broke off, biting her lip.

'And you expected them to stay together, even in those circumstances?'

'They could have *tried*.' She said it forcefully, her hands balled into fists on the table.

'Maybe they did try. Maybe they tried as hard as they knew how for the first six years of your life,' he answered roughly.

Stubbornly she shook her head. 'I don't believe that. I don't think they thought about me at all.'

'For God's sake grow up!' Guy exclaimed, suddenly impatient. 'You can't expect two people who've grown to hate each other to stay married, even when there's a child to consider. It wouldn't be fair on any of them, least of all the child. Surely you're adult enough to see that? To go on resenting the fact as you've done is both childish and incredibly stupid,' he told her roundly.

Michelle's cheeks flushed with anger as she got hastily to her feet. 'How dare you talk to me like that? That's the second time today you've told me to grow up. What do you see yourself as—a surrogate father or something? You're certainly old enough to be my father!' she added nastily.

If anything she expected him to be angry at her rudeness, but to her surprise he just laughed mockingly. 'That's just the kind of reaction I'd expect from a kid like you.'

'You beast! I'm not a kid.'

She lunged at him, fists flying, and Guy put his hands up to protect his face, still laughing.

'You swine! Stop it. Stop laughing at me!' She hit out at him wildly with her fists, sending a glass flying from the table to shatter on the floor. One or two blows landed on his chest, but then he'd caught her wrists and twisted them behind her. Furiously Michelle tried to kick him and to butt him with her head, but he pulled her hard down on to his knee and imprisoned her legs between his. Her wrists he gripped in his right hand and his left he coiled in her long hair, forcing her to be still.

He wasn't laughing now, his jaw was thrust forward and his mouth was set in a hard line. 'You spoilt brat! Someone should have put you over their knee and given you a good spanking years ago.'

'Acting the heavy father again?' she demanded sneeringly, then winced with annoyance as he pulled her hair.

'Maybe I ought to at that. I'd certainly be doing both of us a favour.'

Furiously Michelle tried to break free, arching her back and trying to pull her arms apart. Guy let her struggle, watching her sardonically until she realised that it was futile and gave up at last. She glared at him malevolently, hating him more at that moment than ever before. 'You pig! You rotten bastard!' she swore at him.

Immediately she was jerked forward so that she fell down over his knee, her legs still imprisoned between his. Letting go of her wrists, he pulled up her tee-shirt. She knew what was going to happen and gave a cry of protest which quickly changed to one of rage as he brought his hand down on her behind. He went on, holding her down as she struggled convulsively, yelling with anger and rage. He held back, not using all the strength of his arm, but the hurt scorched through the thin seat of her pants. Only when her yells and expletives ceased and he could feel her shaking with bitten back sobs did he stop and let her go.

'You asked for that,' he told her, grim-faced and breathing rather heavily.

Michelle didn't look at him, she just scrambled to her feet and ran out of the galley, to lock herself in her cabin and throw herself on her bunk, tears of rage and humiliation running down her face. No one, not even her own parents, had ever dared to lay a finger on her before. God, how she hated him, hated him! She lay on the bunk in the darkness, engulfed in self-pity, and it was a long time before she could even begin to acknowledge that maybe she had asked for it, that by swearing at him like that she had got no more than she deserved. Gingerly she got off the bunk and put on the light so that she could examine herself in the mirror. The marks of his hand were clearly to be seen, and she shivered, remembering the ease with which he had held her, even though she had struggled so hard to break free. The strength in his big frame was enormous compared to her own. He had only to exert it to make her do anything he wanted.

Gradually it dawned on her that she had deliberately provoked him into a reaction, but not the one she had subconsciously wanted. Held like that, between his knees, feeling him so close to her, she had wanted an excuse to 'get even closer, to touch him, and so she had tried to fight him. In all the romantic films she had ever seen a fight had always ended with the man taking the girl in his arms and kissing her passionately, but Guy, unpredictably, had treated her like a naughty child and put her over his knee. Would he have had the same reaction, she wondered, if she hadn't admitted she was a virgin? Slowly she undressed and got into bed, deciding to lie quietly and think things out for a while. Was he going to treat her like a child for the rest of the voyage? It was comforting to know that she was safe from him, of course, but even so ... Michelle turned on her side, feeling suddenly very hot and pushing off the sleeping-bag. Although Guy had handled her so roughly, he hadn't lost his temper with her; had never, in fact, lost control of his emotions since she'd been on board, and she couldn't help wondering just how much provocation it might take and how he would behave if that iron self-discipline ever broke.

The sun the next morning felt at least ten degrees hotter than the day before and she hardly needed Guy to tell her that they had entered the tropics. She had greeted him warily at breakfast, but he seemed to have the ability to put things completely behind him and his manner was quite normal. After she'd done all the jobs down below, Guy set her to cleaning the main cabin's windows, but the sun was so hot that she soon felt sticky and uncomfortable, her tee-shirt wet with perspiration. Michelle shaded her eyes against the glare and wished heartily for a swimsuit of some kind. Even Guy succumbed to the heat and went down below, to reappear after a few minutes wearing only a pair of denim shorts. She looked at him enviously as he went by and he grinned, guessing her thoughts.

'Never mind, you'll be able to buy yourself some clothes when you get to Bermuda.'

'That'll be great. The things I'm wearing are almost falling apart from being washed so often.'

Which was literally true; for a while Michelle had contemplated using her underwear as a bikini, but the delicate lace was starting to fray and tear away from the silk, and they *were* very thin, transparent almost. No, she had a feeling it would be better not to try it, she would just have to sweat it out in the tee-shirt. At midday she went below to fix a snack lunch and was glad to be in the shade for a while. Afterwards she washed up the dishes and then looked for a clean tea-towel. There were several brand new ones in a drawer, some plain red, some red and white stripes. Seeing them gave her an idea, so, after she'd finished drying up, she took the pair of scissors, needle and white cotton from Guy's very basic sewing kit and began to fashion herself a bikini. It took her a couple of hours and was nowhere near as

neat as it would have been sewn on a machine, but
Michelle was pleased with the finished result. The
bottom half she'd made from a plain red towel and
had been comparatively simple, just shaped and
tying in knots at the sides, but the top half, for which
she'd used the striped material, had been more difficult, but she'd used strips of the material as strings
and was confident it would cover her adequately
without falling down.

Taking off the hated tee-shirt, she put on the bikini
and sauntered nonchalantly out on to the deck. Guy,
as usual, was up on the fly-bridge and had his back
towards her as she came up. He was standing at the
wheel and his legs, long and muscular, were planted
apart on the deck to counteract the movement of the
boat. His legs were as tanned as his chest and he
didn't seem to suffer any discomfort from the heat at
all. He glanced round as she came up to him and his
eyes stayed on her for a second revealing surprise
and something else she didn't have time to fathom,
but then it was gone as he looked at her face.

'I thought you might like a cold beer,' Michelle
offered, holding out the can she'd brought up for
him.

'Thanks. Take the wheel for a moment while I
drink it, will you?'

Surprised that he was willing to let her take charge
of his precious boat for even a minute, Michelle
answered rather nervously, 'But I don't know how.'

'It's quite simple. Look, you just watch the compass here and turn the wheel so that the engines
counteract the movement of the tide and current,
and we stay on the same heading as we are now.
Come and try,' he encouraged her.

Obediently Michelle moved to stand beside him
and gingerly took the wheel in her hands, keeping

her eyes fixedly on the compass, afraid the needle
might move even a degree off the point.

'That's it. Don't turn it too much. Little and often
is the rule.'

He stood watching her, sipping from the can of
beer, and seemed quite unaware of her bikini.
Michelle concentrated hard on her task, but gradually, as she relaxed her rigid grip on the wheel, she
began to feel the life of the boat running through
her fingers; the purring vibration of the engines far
down in the hold below, the slight jar whenever they
smashed through a wave, the pull of the tide and the
pressure of the breeze. A sudden surge of excitement
and power filled her as she felt the boat answer willingly to the commands she gave it. It was so big,
and yet she could handle it. The feeling reminded
her vividly of the time when she'd passed her driving
test and had driven a car alone for the very first
time. The same immensely heady sensation of power
and achievement had filled her then, as if she had
been handed a bright, shining sword with which she
became invincible.

Turning a glowing, laughing face to Guy, she
exclaimed enthusiastically, 'This is great! I had no
idea it was so easy.'

He grinned. 'Got the bug already, have you?
Maybe I'll make a sailor out of you yet—that's if
you ever get to know port from starboard,' he added
drily.

'Teach me,' Michelle commanded, for once
immune to his irony.

Guy looked at her contemplatively, then shrugged.
'Okay. Why not? We'll start from the bow and work
back to the stern.'

Patiently he went over the nautical terms with her,
Michelle repeating them after him. Some were

simple and made sense, but other things had such strange names that she couldn't think how on earth they'd come by them in the first place, but she had a quick, retentive memory and, with the help of mnemonics, got most of the names right when he tested her.

'Very good,' Guy complimented her, then smiled thinly as she grinned with pleasure. 'Don't let it go to your head; we still haven't touched on the engine and steering components, the navigating equipment or the radio yet.'

Michelle laughed. 'They all sound too technical, not about actually sailing at all.'

'Nevertheless no seagoing vessel is without them now, and the more aids you have on a boat the better chance you have of selling.' He had been leaning against the rail, but now he came over to her. 'I'd better take over; your shoulders are starting to colour.' He frowned in thought. 'I'm not sure whether there's any sun-tan oil on board. Have a look in my cabin, but if you can't find any you'll have to use olive oil from the galley.'

'But I'll smell awful,' Michelle objected.

'Better that than getting burnt. And don't stay out in the sun too long the first time. Okay?'

Michelle came to attention and gave him a mock salute. 'Aye, aye, captain.'

He looked at her quickly, then laughed as he turned back to look out to sea again. 'I suppose I asked for that.' Michelle moved to walk away, but stopped as he added, 'By the way, I like the bikini.'

Stepping back so that she could see his face, she said provocatively, 'So you noticed?'

For a moment she didn't think he would answer, but then his head slowly came round until their eyes met and held. 'Yes, I noticed.'

'Guy . . .'

She wasn't sure what she had been going to say, but already he'd turned away. His tone curt and final, he said, 'Go on, go and put on some oil.'

Reluctantly Michelle obeyed him, but forgot the incident for a while as she searched for and found some oil and carried her sleeping bag up to the main deck to lie on while she sunbathed. There was very little breeze where she was lying down because the guardrail was fitted with glass-fibre windshields—what had Guy called them? Dodgers. Yes, that was it—and she could feel the heat burning into her newly exposed skin. Better to do as Guy said and not spend too long out here. She couldn't see him from where she was lying; he was hidden by the super-structure of the main saloon, but she could picture him up there on the bridge, braced against the movement of the sea.

The fact that he had noticed her bikini sent a finger of excitement running through her. And the look he had given her had proved that he was still aware of her sexually, even though he now wasn't prepared to do anything about it. She didn't know much about such things, but she supposed he was a very virile man. Her fiancé Peter and previous boy-friends had seemed to think of little else but sex, and she couldn't see that older men would be that much different, just better able to control their sex drive. Which was lucky for her. She could quite see that being alone with a girl for nearly two weeks could be extremely frustrating for a man. Or vice versa, for that matter.

She turned over and shut her eyes against the glare of the sun. Was that what this continual restlessness she felt was—frustration? Did her body want what her heart and mind forbade? She was certainly old enough, but strangely, apart from a natural curiosity she had never felt any strong desire to go farther than kissing and petting, no violent sexual need to give her body completely. Not that she even wanted that now, not really. But she did wonder what it would be like to go to bed with Guy, to be taken by him. He was very experienced, even she could tell that, and somehow she had an idea that he could make a night spent with him a devastatingly unforgettable experience. And would he then, in those circumstances, unleash his emotions, or would it be just sex? Michelle shivered suddenly, despite the heat; somehow she knew that to go to bed with Guy, knowing that he felt nothing but concupiscence, would be as mentally humiliating an experience as it would be physically satisfying.

Her thoughts went back to their conversation, or argument rather, the previous night when they had been discussing her parents' divorce. He had been vehemently in favour of their splitting up when he heard how badly they had argued. Did that, Michelle wondered, mean that he himself had been married and divorced? He might even be married now for all she knew, although he didn't wear a ring and had never mentioned a wife, and somehow she had never thought of him as being married. But she supposed he could have been in the past, might even have had children. And if the marriage had worked out badly that could account for his complete control of his emotions, his refusal to betray feelings that could still be raw and bleeding from past wounds, perhaps recent wounds even.

'Mitch.'

Guy's voice above her broke starkly into her thoughts and she jumped guiltily. 'Yes, what is it?'

'You've been out there long enough. Either go

and put a shirt on or go below.'

Michelle did as she was told, wondering again if the fact that he treated her like a child meant that he was a father himself.

That night she came right out and asked him. Once the idea had got into her mind she couldn't get rid of it, and she just *had* to know. They were sitting out on the deck, leaning against the wall of the main saloon. The moon was very bright, a perfect silver sphere against the black velvet texture of the night. Star clusters that she didn't recognise hung in the sky and the waves were capped by glowing phosphorescence as they ran and broke across the surface of the dark, empty sea. They sat for some time in a companionable silence, Guy with a rod in his hands but not really worried about catching anything, a tumbler of whisky at his side, while Michelle sipped a cocktail he'd mixed for her which was longer and less potent.

Unable to contain her curiosity any longer, she asked boldly, 'Guy, are you married?'

She saw him stiffen before he said coldly, 'That's a very personal question.'

'Don't try and put me down. It's no more personal than some of those you asked me the other night,' she retorted.

He turned to look at her, but some quirk of the moonlight left his eyes in shadow and she couldn't tell what he was thinking. Abruptly he said, 'No, I'm not married. I never have been.'

'Oh.' She didn't know how to go on, how to ask him what she wanted to know, but luckily he gave her an opening.

'Why wait till now to ask? That's usually the first thing a woman establishes about a man.'

'I only just now began to wonder.'

'To wonder what?'

'To wonder why you're like you are,' she replied inadequately.

'So you're starting to think of someone other than yourself for a change. Maybe you are starting to grow up after all.'

Michelle was about to answer indignantly, but suddenly saw that he was trying to sidetrack her. Determinedly she pursued, 'I wondered why you don't like women very much.'

He laughed mockingly. 'On the contrary, I like women a great deal. You should know that,' he added with deliberate emphasis.

Glad of the darkness to hide the sudden flush that coloured her cheeks, Michelle went on doggedly, 'You may enjoy going to bed with women, but you don't *like* them, not as people. You just treat them as a—as a convenient means of satisfying your needs.'

'Hark at the nineteen-year-old psychiatrist,' he remarked with cold, insulting sarcasm. 'Really, Mitch, you're becoming quite eloquent!'

Michelle bit her lip, unable to speak, feeling suddenly sick and miserable inside and wishing she'd never started this whole thing, wanting to just crawl away and shut herself in her cabin.

But to her astonishment and relief, he went on harshly, 'As you've never seen me with another woman you must mean that I don't like you and treat you only as a means to an end. How can you possibly judge that the way I treat you is the way I treat all women?'

Michelle shrugged. 'I just know, that's all. Call it instinct, if you like?'

'Oh, instinct.' The two words contained total masculine derision.

'Well, don't you?'

He was silent for a long time, then, harshly, 'I admit I have no cause to feel very favourable towards your sex. I was very much   love with a woman once and I wanted to marry her.'

Tentatively Michelle asked, 'What—what happened?'

'Oh, the usual thing. She met someone who could give her far more than I could and went away with him a month before the wedding.' He laughed with bitter irony. 'She even took the wedding presents with her!'

Michelle tried to keep her voice light. 'I believe the stock answer to that is that you were lucky to be rid of her before it was too late.'

He stood up abruptly, tossing the rod on to the deck. 'Which just shows how little you know. But you were right about one thing; I do have very little regard for your sex, and no woman I've met since has made me change that opinion,' he added savagely. Then he turned and strode down the deck to the companionway and disappeared below.

Michelle watched him go, then got up to put the rod away, a strange feeling of intense hatred in her heart for the woman who had hurt him so badly, but all mixed up with envy and jealousy too, because the love he'd given her must have been very great for the hurt and bitterness to have lasted for so long.

CHAPTER SIX

THE next few days were uneventful, Michelle wary of antagonising Guy again and making sure to keep to safe, uncontroversial subjects. He let her take the wheel again and showed her how some of the instruments worked, but most of the time she spent on deck sunbathing or, when that got too much, down below in the welcome air-conditioned coolness of the galley. She began to experiment with various recipes and found that she quite enjoyed cooking after all, now that she had a free hand and plenty of time to work in.

Guy, pleased with the way the boat was performing, had told her that they should reach Bermuda in about forty-eight hours, but late that evening, when he was making his routine radio call to England, the note of the engines altered, became irregular, and then ground to a halt. Michelle had been cleaning up in the galley and had to get quickly out of the way as Guy came rushing through to throw open a hatch in the floor of the corridor and disappear down it.

'What is it? What's happened?' Michelle came to stand at the edge of the hatch and peer down.

'The engines have seized.' Guy's voice came up to her from the bottom of a stainless steel ladder as he began to inspect the engines. 'Go to my cabin and bring me an overall, would you?'

She did so and climbed down the ladder to give it to him, looking round her interestedly while he put it on. The area was far different from what she had expected; in films engine rooms were always dark, greasy areas of noise and heat, but that on the *Ethos* was almost clinically clean with all the walls and most of the engine parts, too, painted white. The ceiling was high enough for Michelle to stand upright, but Guy was too tall, he had to stoop all the time, but the place was well lit and he had no difficulty in examining the engines.

'What do you think it is?'

'Don't know yet.' He was looking at a clear-plastic covered sort of window and then moved on to another one nearer the engines. 'Ah, I thought so.' He gave an exclamation of satisfaction. 'The filter leading to the engine cooling intake is blocked.'

'Can you clear it?'

'Yes, quite easily. But it caused the engines to overheat, so I'll have to check that it didn't do any damage.'

He began to whistle rather tunelessly as he worked and Michelle perched on a rung of the ladder, watching him and marvelling at the adroitness of his hands and the skill which could make sense of all the bits of the engines which had taken him unerringly to the cause of the trouble, and which were a complete mystery to her.

'Hmm, that's unfortunate. The heat's buckled part of the exhaust manifold. I'll have to replace it with a new one.'

'Really?' Michelle said politely. 'Will it take long?'

He looked up at her and grinned, knowing that she hadn't understood a word. 'About an hour or so, I should think.'

Soon the heat built up in the small area and Guy left a dark streak of oil across his forehead as he wiped away the drops of perspiration that were threatening to run into his eyes. After about half an hour Michelle, without being asked, climbed back up the ladder and got him a can of cold beer from the fridge in the galley.

'Thanks.' There were pieces of engine lying round his feet as Guy took the beer from her, straightened up to drink it and banged his head on the ceiling. She laughed at him as he swore ruefully, but then both of them froze into stunned silence as the piercing note of the alarm system sounded throughout the boat.

Guy recovered first, dropping the can of beer and springing to the other side of the engine room. 'Get up to the wheelhouse!' he shouted at her sharply. 'Turn on all the other lights and those in the main saloon as you go, and switch the emergency horn on and leave it on. Then get a life vest from the wheelhouse and put it on, and put as much food and drink in the dinghy as you have time for. Stay by the dinghy with a sharp knife and if whatever's out there gets close, get in the dinghy and cut it free.'

'But what about you?'

'Just do as I say. Don't wait for me. Lord, this would have to happen when we're adrift.' He was working feverishly as he snapped out the orders, doing something Michelle couldn't see with some electrical wires.

'But I can't just leave you!' she gasped, fear and distress in her voice.

He turned his head and yelled at her. 'For God's sake stop arguing and get going!'

She turned then and flew up the steps, through the galley and up into the main saloon, remembering somehow to switch on the lights as she went. In the wheelhouse the sound of the alarm was almost deafening and she could see the blip on the radar screen as the needle of light traced endlessly back and forwards. With a sob of pure frustration, she looked at the instrument panel in despair. How on earth was she supposed to know which was the horn and extra lights? She half turned to run back down to Guy to ask him, but as she did so she looked through the starboard window and saw several lights seemingly suspended over the sea about four miles or so away. For a second she couldn't think what they were, but then, to her appalled horror, she realised that they were the lights of a big ship, its decks and superstructure high over the waterline. God, it was huge! And it was heading straight for them! Desperately her eyes ran over the seemingly endless knobs, dials and switches on the control panel. A label over one read 'AUXILIARY LIGHTS' and she pushed the button frantically. Immediately the decks were ablaze with light, and a huge bulb, almost as brilliant as a searchlight, began to slowly turn at the masttop, its powerful beam cutting through the night. Michelle gave a gasp of relief, soon lost as she sought frantically for the horn. At last, after what seemed like light years, she found the button in the panel set into the bulkhead almost above her head. Thankfully she pressed it and heard its comforting howl surge stridently across the sea.

As she ran back to the galley she glanced again at the ship. It seemed much nearer already, now she could make out the darker mass of the hull against the darkness of the sea. Gasping with mingled terror and exertion, she began to carry food and bottles of drink from the galley to the dinghy, choosing haphazardly and continually glancing over her shoulder at the ship, the life vest she had hastily pulled on impeding her and getting in the way. Surely, surely the ship must see or hear them. If there was anyone on deck, if they weren't all below. For an instant she had a brief but very vivid mental picture of the ship's crew, down below in well-lit cabins, eating, playing cards perhaps, all chatting and laughing to one another as they travelled on, unaware of the danger and threat they represented.

Scrabbling in the cutlery drawer, Michelle found a carving knife, unaware that she had cut her fingers in the process. She turned to go and stand by the dinghy as she'd been told, but then gave a sob of terror and ran instead down the corridor to the engine room hatch.

'Guy, it's a ship, a big one! And it's still coming on. I'm sure it hasn't seen us.' Her words were broken by panting, gasping sobs and she stared down at him in as much terror as she would have stared down into the pit of hell.

He was still working away in the corner and his tone seemed quite calm as he said, 'Have you done everything I told you to?'

'Yes. Yes. *Come on!* What are you *doing*?'

'Then go back to the dinghy. When the ship gets to within half a mile cut the ropes and row as far away from the boat as you can. Do you understand?'

'No. I'm not going without you.' The words came out quite involuntarily, she hadn't had to think about them at all.

Guy's eyes never left his task, but he rapped out forcefully, 'You'll do as you're damn well told! Now get out of here and get back to the dinghy.'

Anger flared through her, an anger born of abject fear and consternation. 'Don't you yell at me, Guy Farringdon!' she shouted back at him. 'I'm not leaving this boat without you and that's final!'

For a split second his eyes came up to look at her

before returning to his task, then to her amazement she saw his mouth curl into a twisted sort of grin.

'For God's sake, this isn't funny,' she stormed at him. 'Will you *please* come out of there?' Her voice rose, very close to hysteria.

'Mitch,' Guy answered almost conversationally, 'be a good girl and do as I ask. I can take care of myself, you know.'

'Oh, Guy.' She stared at him helplessly.

Again his eyes looked briefly up at her. 'Please, darling,' he said firmly.

She hesitated for only a second longer, then turned with a sob and ran out on to the deck again. The ship, an oil tanker, was much closer now, apparently still unaware of their presence because it was still on the same course. Michelle could make out the huge, towerlike structure towards the stern of the tanker now, the bright squares of light from the windows streaming out into the darkness. Oh, please, please make somebody see, somebody hear! She couldn't tell how far away it was; by day distances were deceptive at sea because you could see for such a long way, at night she found them almost impossible. But it was close, very close.

With a little moan of despair, she climbed into the dinghy and held the knife against the ropes. She went to slash through the first one, but something held her back and she couldn't do it. Biting her lip, she raised the knife again, determined this time. Guy had said he could take care of himself, she had to trust him. But just then the thunderous blast of a ship's hooter tore through the night, drowning out the sound of their own horn as if it was the cheep of a bird. The ship had seen them! Oh, thank goodness!

Michelle heaved a great sigh of relief and climbed

back on deck, throwing off the cumbersome life vest and running to the wheelhouse to send answering bursts on the *Ethos'* hooter, expecting to see the ship slow down and change course, but nothing seemed to be happening; it was still bearing down on them, although the siren-like sound of the hooter still blared out across the sea. She stared as it gradually grew nearer, held in a sort of frozen immobility, fascinated by the sheer size of the great ship as its bows surged towards them through the water.

The great steel hull was only two hundred yards away and Michelle was looking *up* at it, when she was suddenly pushed bodily to one side as Guy ran into the wheelhouse. He did something to the controls, his hands working at frenzied speed, and then, most fantastically wonderful of all sounds, the engines burst into throbbing life. He threw the wheel hard over to port, opened the throttles to their full extent and they surged through the sea, seemingly almost scraping under the bows of the supertanker. The wash of the ship crashed against the sides of the boat and threw it about worse than any storm, but then they were through and Guy reached out to turn off the horn and the alarm system, leaving only the angry, remonstrative sound of the ship's siren to break the blessed silence.

Guy slowed down the engine and said casually, 'Sorry, that was a mite close.'

'Close?' Michelle turned on him furiously. 'We were almost killed! They didn't even see us till the last minute, and even then they didn't slow down or stop.'

'They couldn't,' Guy replied. 'A ship that size takes at least a mile in which to stop or change course. We were lucky she saw us at all, a small boat adrift at night. If she hadn't seen us we'd have been just another boat that disappeared without trace in the Bermuda Triangle.'

'The Bermuda Triangle?' Michelle stared at him in horror, then tried to take a grip on herself. 'How did you get the engines going?'

'I didn't. There's another, outboard, engine in case of emergency, but I had to wire it up to the battery generator before it would work.'

'You mean you were risking your life to do that when you could have got away in the dinghy? What if you'd been too late?'

'It was worth the risk; I had a rough idea of how long I'd got and I just had to work fast, that's all. Besides, this baby's too valuable to chance losing without a fight,' he added, patting the steering wheel.

'Why, you ... you ...' Words failed her. 'All you care about is your rotten boat! It doesn't matter to you that we were nearly killed, does it?' she raged at him. 'You wouldn't have stood a chance if the tanker had hit the boat. Even if you'd survived the impact you'd have been drowned in the wash. You're crazy! You're just stupid and crazy and ...'

'Hey, hold on.' Guy took hold of her arms and gently drew her to him as he felt the tremors of shock and fear running through her body. 'I'm not the only crazy one, am I? Why didn't you get away in the dinghy when you had the chance?'

She didn't answer him, not knowing herself why she hadn't. She pressed close to his warmth and strength, feeling suddenly cold and shivery. His arms tightened around her, giving comfort and security. Slowly the shivering stopped and she became aware of the closeness of his body against her own. Her nostrils were filled with the manly smell of him as she stirred in his arms, fingers of sensuality spreading through her.

Slowly she lifted her head. 'Guy . . .'

'It's all right, it's all over now.'

He bent his head to speak to her, his face only a few inches away. Michelle's lips parted as she stretched towards him. His lips touched hers gently, a kiss of comfort, no more. For a moment she was content with that, content to feel the soft tenderness of his lips gently touching hers, but then a fierce hunger swept through her and she put her arms round his neck, pushing her lips against his and opening her mouth to kiss him with a sudden, almost desperate, longing.

Guy's hands tightened on her back, pressing into her flesh and hurting her. His mouth took hers greedily, with passion and abandon, heating the fire within her into a fierce, consuming flame. She pressed herself even closer against him, moving sensuously, feeling his body harden in response. Michelle moaned, a deepfelt cry of physical need. She was on fire with desire, with a desperate craving for fulfilment.

Her own emotions so engulfed her that she was hardly aware that Guy had suddenly grown still. He made a sound, half groan, half exclamation, deep in his throat, and then his hands were at her arms, pulling them from round his neck, pushing her away.

'No!' Michelle gave a moan of protest and tried to get back in his embrace, but he held her rigidly at arm's length, his breathing uneven, thin beads of sweat on his brow. For a moment they stared at each other in the moonlight, Michelle's heart gradually slowing as the world stopped spinning and she became aware of her surroundings.

'Guy . . .' She looked at him beseechingly, wanting

reassurance, wanting ... not really knowing what she wanted, but feeling a desperate need for him to understand; out of his manhood and wider experience to find and give her the means to see and cope with what had happened to her.

But there was anger in his face and in his tone as he pushed her roughly, almost violently away and exclaimed, 'You little fool! Don't you know what the hell you're doing to me?' His hands bunched into fists at his sides and he turned abruptly away. 'I'll go and finish fixing the main engines. You'd better unload the dinghy again.'

And then he was gone, leaving her alone in the wheelhouse to try and fight the waves of frustration that rose to torment her, to still the tremors of awareness that left her raw and vulnerable.

It was some time before Michelle moved to obey him, and even then she wasn't fully in control of herself, her hands still a little unsteady as she unloaded the dinghy. If she hadn't been so upset she might have laughed at the assortment of things she'd grabbbed in her panic: bottles of whisky and gin instead of water or minerals, and tins of cake and packets of chocolate biscuits instead of something more practical and substantial. Well, she thought with a flash of rueful satire, if I had left in the dinghy and managed to reach land at least I'd have arrived fat and drunk! The idea made her want to laugh, but somehow she wanted to cry too. She sat down on the step leading from the saloon to the deck feeling hopelessly perplexed and confused, floundering in a crazy mixture of emotions that frightened and yet fascinated her at the same time, which was more or less the same feelings that she had about Guy. She knew that it had been stupid to throw herself at him like that, that she'd been playing with fire, but she couldn't help it, there was no way she could have stopped herself. After that terrible ten minutes of impending disaster from which he had saved her, some primeval instinct had made her turn to him—for comfort, in gratitude, or just because they were still alive and safe—she didn't know. All she did know, with any certainty, was that in those few moments of their embrace she had experienced an emotion more violent and urgent than any she had ever known, one which had engulfed sanity and pride and carried her down into a swirling whirlpool of passion. Only to have it thrown back in her face as he had pushed her away.

She was still sitting on the step when Guy emerged from the engine room, wiping his hands on a piece of rag, a damp patch on the front of the white boiler suit where perspiration had soaked through. He paused when he saw her and eyed her a little warily as he came nearer. Then he saw the bottle of gin cradled in her arms.

'Have you been drinking that?' he demanded sharply.

'What? Oh, no.' She shook her head. 'It was one of the things I loaded into the dinghy. I put the craziest things in there.' He bent and took the bottle from her, put it away in a cupboard, without comment. 'Guy, I'm—I'm sorry.' She forced herself to look at him.

'Put it down to the heat of the moment,' he answered lightly, but then, his voice changing, he added abruptly, 'You don't make it any easier.'

Michelle's eyes widened. 'Do you mean you . . .'

'I don't mean anything,' he interrupted tersely. 'Go to bed, I'll put the rest of the things away.'

For a moment Michelle stiffened, ready to defy him, but then she shrugged and stood up. There was

no point in arguing, and he was right; after the peak
of fear and tension she now felt drained and exhausted and would be better off in bed. Away from
Guy, his closeness and the disturbing feelings that
closeness inspired.

She woke the next morning in a strangely contrary
mood, one minute on top of the world, laughing and
singing, the next strangely uptight, close to tears and
wanting to hit out viciously at something, *anything*!
Fortunately Guy was up ahead of her and had made
his own breakfast, she couldn't have faced standing
over the cooker in this heat. The sun sweltered down
from a cloudless blue sky, but it was a humid heat,
quite unlike the dry heat of the Mediterranean
countries. Michelle did her chores automatically by
now, becoming more efficient every day, so that she
was out on the deck sunbathing by ten o'clock.
Luckily she'd had a faint tan left over from last year
when she had spent a couple of weeks at a villa in
the south of France that belonged to one of her
mother's admirers. Then the man had become more
than just an admirer and she'd been sent home out
of the way. By now her skin was turning a very satis-
factory golden colour and she could spend quite long
periods in the sun without burning.

But today was especially humid, she could feel it
as soon as she walked on deck and within half an
hour she was soaked with perspiration. She thought
of getting herself a drink, but knew that she would
only feel thirsty again ten minutes later. The top
half of her bikini was wet with sweat, the edges of
the thick material rubbing her armpits every time
she moved and making them sore. Reaching behind
her, she untied the strings and lay down again on
her front. That was better, it was much looser now
and didn't rub so much. And besides, she would be

able to brown the pale mark where the strap had been.

Guy passed her several times as he went from the flying bridge down to the engine room, checking on his work last night, she supposed. He was wearing the usual pair of denim shorts, his legs and top half tanned a deep, dark brown. He was whistling as he worked and taking no notice of her. In fact he had hardly taken any notice of her at all today except to say good morning and that he didn't want breakfast. A growing sense of resentment filled her; how *could* he be so offhand, act as if nothing had happened between them? Did he have to so obviously display the fact that he was immune to her proximity? But then Michelle remembered his remark last night— that she didn't make things any easier. Did that mean, she wondered, that she had come close to breaking his iron resolve?

She let her mind drift back, remembering the way he had returned her kiss for a few crushing seconds before he had thrust her angrily away. Wondering what would have happened if . . . if . . . She stirred and lifted her hair off the back of her neck. It was hot, so hot. She sat up, holding the bikini top against her. From here she could see Guy sitting at the controls of the flying-bridge, sunglasses shielding his eyes as he gazed out to sea, but although they had sighted one or two ships in the distance that day, they were still far enough away from Bermuda for the horizon to be empty.

The idea came to her when Michelle remembered all the girls she'd seen sunbathing topless in France. There it had been an accepted thing, with only a few lascivious men or pop-eyed boys to spoil the naturalness of it. But here, on the *Ethos*? She looked up at Guy's uncommunicative back view and decided that he wouldn't approve. If she'd been the kind of girl he'd first thought her, then she could probably have sunbathed completely nude for all he cared, but since he'd found out that she was a virgin his attitude had changed radically. Now—a thrill of fascinated temptation filled her—now it would be interesting to see whether she could *prove* that he wasn't immune to her. Casting the bikini top aside, Michelle lay down where Guy could see her if he looked round.

She closed her eyes. Mmm, it felt good! She had never exposed her breasts to the sun before. Sensuous pleasure was mixed with nervous anticipation. What would Guy do when he saw? She felt at once brazen and frightened to death. But she had to prove to herself that he really found her attractive, wanted her despite the self-imposed barriers that he'd put up. In the beginning he'd said he'd only wanted her because she was female and available, not caring about her at all, but now, if he wanted her now despite himself, then surely that must prove that he cared a little? Opening her eyes, she sneaked a look up at the fly-bridge; Guy was still sitting with his back to her, facing out to sea. Michelle closed her eyes again and began to doze in the sun.

'What the hell are you trying to do?'

Guy's grim voice close by brought her instantly awake. He was standing beside her, towering over her, hands on his hips, his body cutting out the sun and casting a dark shadow across her legs. Michelle's heart began to beat erratically, but she managed to look up at him without betraying it.

'Oh, hello, Guy,' she stretched voluptuously, 'I must have fallen asleep. Is it time for lunch?'

'You heard me,' he repeated harshly. 'What are you trying to do?'

Michelle put her hand up to shield her eyes and thought of pretending not to understand him, but one look at his steely cold grey eyes made her change her mind. 'Trying to get an even tan, of course.'

'Put the top back on,' he commanded, picking up the bikini and tossing it to her.

It landed by her left hand, but she made no attempt to pick it up. Instead she pouted up at him. 'Oh, Guy, don't be so old-fashioned! All the girls sunbathe topless nowadays.'

'Not on this boat they don't. Put it on, Mitch.'

She gazed back at him defiantly. 'No, I won't.'

His eyes narrowed and her heart skipped a beat, afraid of what he might do. So she was almost disappointed when, after a moment, he merely said mildly, 'You'll burn up.'

Pushed into recklessness, Michelle answered thickly, 'So why don't you put some sun-tan lotion on for me?'

She thought his jaw tightened, but he gave no other sign whatsoever as he said equably, 'All right. Stand up.'

Slowly, keeping her eyes on his face, Michelle picked up the bottle of oil and got to her feet. Silently he took the bottle from her and unscrewed the cap, poured some of the oil into his hand. Michelle's pulse began to race as she waited for him to touch her, her eyes still on his face, afraid to look down at his hand. His mouth was set into a thin line, but his eyes were completely impassive. He turned aside to set the bottle down and then turned back to her. Suddenly she was afraid again and had to look away.

Her skin was already hot, but even so his fingers seemed to burn into her as he cupped her left breast and slowly began to massage in the oil, his hand moving almost rhythmically around the high, firm peak. And then his other hand was there too, spreading the oil, making her stifle a gasp of pleasure. It was the most wonderfully sensuous experience she'd ever known. She glanced down under her lashes and saw his hands at work on her, saw her own breasts, pale against her tan, harden under the manipulation of his strong, firm hands. A wave of sheer yearning, more violent than anything she had felt before, shook her, she gasped and turned her head to him, her face naked and vulnerable with desire.

The cold, almost bored look on Guy's face acted like a bucket of cold water being thrown in her face. For a moment she couldn't believe that touching her had no effect on him at all when it was doing such wonderful things to her, but then she quickly stepped away and turned her back on him, her heart beating painfully.

'Enough?' he asked calmly.

'Yes. Yes, thanks.' She managed to answer although her voice stuck in her throat.

'I'll get back on the bridge, then.'

He turned away, but she stopped him before he began to climb the ladder. 'Guy . . .' there was a note of entreaty in her voice.

'Yes?'

Instinctively her hands covered her breasts as she looked at him. 'I . . . I . . .'

'Well?' But she couldn't go on and his mouth twisted mockingly. 'What's the matter, Mitch? Why so afraid all of a sudden? You were confident enough a moment ago.'

'I know, but I . . .' It was no good, she couldn't put it into words.

He came back to stand beside her, lifted his arms suddenly and pulled her hands away from her breasts.

'No!' She gave a cry of protest.

'What's the matter? You were eager enough to flaunt them in front of me before. Why cover them up now?'

'Don't.' She tried to break free, but his hands were like steel bands circling her wrists. 'Please, Guy, don't!'

'Why not?' he insisted.

'Because ... because it's different now.' She mumbled out the words, afraid to look at him.

'Different? Why? Because your little ploy to try and provoke me didn't work? Did you really think I was going to go berserk or something at the sight of them?' he demanded scornfully. 'My God, you're naïve! I may have been at sea a long time, but not that long.'

Tears of humiliation came to her eyes and she tried to wrench herself free. 'Stop it! Let me go.'

But his voice continued, coldly and cruelly. 'It's not as if I hadn't seen them before.' Deliberately he pushed her wrists back behind her and let his eyes dwell on her breasts, the oil on them making them glisten like gold in the sunlight. 'Your breasts aren't bad,' he told her brutally, 'quite a good shape, in fact, but let's face it, Mitch, when you've seen one woman you've seen them all. And it hardly matters what shape they are in when they're in ...'

But Michelle had heard enough. With a supreme effort she wrenched herself free of his hands and with a sob of shame and humiliation she ran down through the galley and along to her cabin, to lock herself in and weep out her mortification on the pillow.

Later she dropped into a deep sleep and didn't awaken until she heard Guy moving around in the galley late that evening. Then she went into the bathroom to shower, carefully washing off what was left of the oil, trying not to think about it. When she went into the galley, dressed in his tee-shirt and jeans, Guy hardly glanced at her, instead nodding towards the window.

'Go up on deck and take a look,' he told her.

Automatically she obeyed him and clutched at the rail in surprise as she saw clustering pinpoints of light strung along the western horizon.

Guy had followed her and she turned to him in some agitation. 'What is it? Are they ships?'

'No. It's the Bermudan Islands. See that larger cluster towards the right? That's Bermuda itself. We'll heave to here for the night and go in on the morning tide.'

He waited for her to say something, but when she didn't he shrugged and went below again.

Michelle stayed on deck for a long time gazing at the lights, realising that their voyage had come to an end at last. At the beginning when her hatred of Guy had been at its height, she had actively longed for this moment, and this afternoon, when she had made such a fool of herself, she had wanted it then; to be able to walk away and never see him again. But now, now that the moment had come? She searched her emotions, looking for relief at being free of the close confines of the *Ethos*, of being free of Guy and his arrogant masculinity for ever. But she could find none, relief just wasn't there. She tried to find the satisfaction she had expected to feel when she revealed her identity and her parents came to collect her. But that too was missing. She recognised now that she had been childish and stupid, that her parents would have to be told and that they had a right to be angry, but somehow that was immaterial.

She thought of her fiancé and realised that it was the first time she'd thought of him in days. Her face flushed with guilt at the understanding of what her foolishness had done to those people who cared for her, but at least she understood it at last. Maybe Guy's rough and ready methods had forced her to do some growing up on this voyage after all.

Would he be relieved that they'd reached their destination? she wondered. He had taken her on with much different plans in mind than teaching a spoilt teenager how to grow up. But he had taught her some salutary lessons, today's being perhaps one of the most important. And just by being with him, she had learned a lot about men. In fact she felt a whole lot older and wiser than she had two weeks ago. She could steer a boat and cook a palatable meal, she knew how to clean quickly and efficiently and she could manufacture a bikini out of a couple of tea-towels. That last made her think again of this afternoon, and it was strange that remembering that made her aware, quite suddenly and definitely, that she wasn't going to marry Peter, that she had never loved him and had only got engaged to him because he offered an escape from her old life. Just as much of an escape as persuading Guy to take her on this voyage had been.

The decision made, Michelle expected to feel a great lifting of her spirits, but the lights of Bermuda were still close, still lighting her way to her last day on the *Ethos*. A sense of loss, almost of desolation, filled her and she gripped the rail hard, not wanting to leave, not ever wanting to leave. Realisation that she was in love with Guy, and that it was him she didn't want to leave, came slowly. It crept into her mind and grew, to fill it with joyful wonder. So that was what her restlessness and crazy moods had all

been about? She was in love with the man and
hadn't even realised it! A tremendous, glowing happiness filled her, and with it came a great sense of
peace and rightness. It didn't matter that Guy had
spurned her cruelly that very day, that he had given
no sign of caring for her. The worries and the fears
would come later; right now all she wanted or
needed was to lose herself, to drown deeply, in this,
the most magical emotion of her young life.

CHAPTER SEVEN

AFTER so long on the open sea, the last few miles into Bermuda seemed to be thronged with traffic. Two large cruise liners passed them on their way home to America from the island, the decks thronged with casually dressed holidaymakers, some of whom waved to them as they passed. There were small cargo boats sailing to and from the various islands and several fast motorboats heading for the open sea to spend the day in trying to catch blue and white marlins or perhaps, if they were lucky, a great barracuda. As they turned into the vast bay formed by the various islands there were also ferryboats to contend with, plying between the main harbour at Hamilton, the capital of Bermuda, and across the bay to the smaller islands forming the north-western peninsula of the bay.

Guy navigated between and around the traffic with efficient confidence and still had time to point out the various places of interest they passed. Michelle had gone to stand at his side on the flying-bridge as soon as they'd finished breakfast, drawn there like a magnet, and trying in vain to keep the happiness and excitement out of her face. But luckily Guy must have put it down to the thrill of reaching Bermuda and made no comment.

The lush greenness of the land seemed strange after the continuous blueness of sea and sky. There were houses along the beaches and set into the hills, painted in bright pastel colours, pink mostly, with white roofs that sparkled in the sun, like icing on a birthday cake. Guy pointed out to her the tall tower of the lighthouse on Gibb's Hill, but they turned to the left before they got near it and began to thread their way through the maze of shipping, both pleasure and commercial, that filled Hamilton Harbour.

Guy cut the engines right down and they slid slowly through the plethora of pleasure craft towards the mooring that Guy had already arranged over the radio.

'There are so many boats here that Bermuda has the nickname "Land of Water",' he told her with a grin.

'Have you been here many times before?'

'Quite a few. I was anchored here quite often when I was in the Navy.'

She looked at him in surprise. 'I didn't know you were in the Navy. Why did you leave?'

He grinned. 'I didn't always take kindly to discipline.'

Michelle smiled with him; she could well imagine him fretting for the freedom to sail where and when he pleased, to have his own deck under his feet instead of having to obey the commands of others.

'Why did you join, then?'

He shrugged. 'I come from a Naval family; it was expected of me. I tried to stick it out, but . . .' he shrugged again, 'I suppose I just prefer small boats to large ones.' Changing the subject abruptly, he lifted his hand to point towards the land. 'See that building up on the hill? That's the Cathedral. And those pink, Italian-looking towers farther along belong to the Sessions House.'

'Are those shops along by the harbour?'

'Yes, that's Front Street.' Guy saw the hungry expression on her face and laughed. 'Don't worry, you'll be able to buy some clothes.' He carefully steered them between a rusty, fussing little cargo boat heading out to sea and an anchored motor-yacht, then told her to go down to the bow and stand by with the rope.

Michelle did as she was told and stood with the breeze lifting her hair, bleached to a lighter shade by the sun, and blowing it back from her head. She could see the harbour clearly now, the traffic along the main road that was directed by a white-uniformed policeman standing on a sort of high bird-cage structure in the intersection, the numerous horses and carriages grouped together under the lush shade of tall palm trees, and the groups of tourists boarding lines of taxis waiting for them at the foot of the gangplanks of the two huge cruise liners that were moored right alongside the dock, their giant superstructures casting thick blocks of shadow over the main road itself.

But Guy steered the boat into a marina just before the dock where there were a great many other visiting boats moored, and Michelle threw the rope to a boy who made it fast. They were there, the long voyage from France was over.

She expected Guy to go ashore at once, but he spent some time fussing over the boat and making sure it was properly moored first. Whereas once this would have annoyed Michelle and made her impatient, now she saw that it was simply attention to detail, the wish for his boat, his creation, to be shown off to perfection. And, of course, he didn't let her sit idly by; he found her a dozen different jobs to do before he was through.

He nodded in grudging satisfaction at last. 'Okay, I think she'll do. I'll get changed now and go and check in at Customs, then I'll go and contact the

broker I deal with here. I don't expect he'll be able
to come and look her over right away, but he might.
If he can't I'll go up to the Post Office on Queen
Street and collect your passport so that you can go
ashore and buy some clothes.'

Michelle looked hastily away, then covered it by
saying, 'Can't I come with you?'

Guy shook his head. 'No. Not until you have your
passport.' He glanced at his watch. 'I'd better get a
move on.'

He disappeared below, leaving Michelle to hang
on the rail and stare out at the busy scene in the
harbour. She had often been abroad before with her
mother, of course, but they had always flown to their
destination because of her mother's busy schedule;
never before had she approached a country by sea,
and somehow she found it infinitely more exciting.
To see the blur on the horizon grow into individual
islands, to make out hills and trees, then the individual buildings, and finally the people, going busily
about their lives, quite unaware of the new boat that
had slipped quietly into their harbour. There were a
great many people wearing Bermuda shorts, and it
seemed very strange to Michelle's eyes to see smart
dark-suited businessmen with briefcases tucked
under their arms and their legs bare below the
knees!

But it seemed even stranger when Guy came up
on deck again twenty minutes later, also dressed in a
crisp grey suit, his shirt startlingly white against his
tanned skin, a striped tie knotted at his neck. He
looked a different person from the man who had
stood at the helm a short time ago in his faded and
rather frayed denim shorts and nothing else.

His eyebrows rose sardonically as he saw her staring at him in open-mouthed astonishment. 'Your

mouth looks like a Venus flytrap looking for food,'
he informed her tartly.

Hastily Michelle shut her mouth, but she was still
bug-eyed as she watched him walk purposefully
ashore. And she wasn't the only one of that opinion;
she saw several people turn to look at his tall, broad
figure as he passed, and the other pedestrians seemed
to make way for him, instinctively moving aside as
he approached, his self-confident bearing carrying
him quickly through the crowds on the jetty until he
was lost to sight by the Customs shed. Michelle found
that her throat had gone tight and that she'd been
gripping the rail hard. She took a deep breath and
let go, but the memory of his big, muscular body
was still there in her mind. How strange that it
should affect her more when he was fully clothed
than when he was in just shorts. Perhaps it was because she'd never seen him in anything but casual
clothes before, never imagined that he could look so
devastatingly urbane and attractive.

Thinking of him drove everything else from her
mind for quite a while, but eventually, and reluctantly, she dragged her thoughts back to her own
affairs. She had no doubt whatsoever that Guy was
going to be mad as fire when he found out that no
passport had arrived for her. He was going to start
demanding explanations and she had better make
up her mind before he came back on just what she
was going to tell him. All she did know for sure was
that she had no intention of telling him the truth,
because then he would send her back to England
willy-nilly, no matter how much she wanted to stay.
And she did want to stay with him, wanted it desperately. It didn't matter that he had been cruel to
her, didn't matter that he showed no sign whatsoever
of caring for her even a little; she clung to the hope

that if she could only stay with him, then somehow, some time he might come to care about her in return. So she would go on bluffing her way along and pretend that she had no idea why her passport hadn't arrived. She smiled to herself gleefully; and there was nothing he could do about it; if the authorities wouldn't let her ashore without a passport then Guy would have to keep her with him until she finally told him the truth or he took her back to England.

But there was still the problem of her parents. For almost the first time, Michelle's conscience smote her; she had never intended that the game would go on as long as this when she had persuaded Guy to take her with him, and had fully intended to end it in Bermuda, but now she had to find a way of letting her parents know that she was safe without giving away her whereabouts. The answer, she found, was simple. She merely sat down and wrote three short letters: one to each of her parents stating that she was quite safe but didn't intend to come home yet, and the third, most difficult letter, to Peter, telling him that her feelings had changed and that she no longer wished to marry him. They all sounded rather curt and she was sorry about that, but there was so much that she didn't want them to know that she was afraid of giving something away if she wrote too much. The letters done, she stole some English money that she found in a drawer in Guy's cabin and gave it to the Bermudan boy who had helped them tie up and who was still lounging on the jetty. She asked him to stamp the letters for her and to send them surface mail. She stressed the surface mail bit because she didn't want the letters to arrive before the *Ethos* was safely out of Bermuda and on the way to America. She watched the boy rather worriedly as he unconcernedly pocketed the money and wandered off towards the town as if being asked to do something like this was commonplace. She just hoped that he was honest and would do as she asked, but there was no alternative when she couldn't leave the boat herself.

It was very late before Guy came back. Michelle was sitting on the deck watching for him, his sweater pulled over the tee-shirt because the breeze had turned cool now that it was dark. The town seemed so busy and so noisy after the quietness of the open sea; music came from the open doors of several bars along the waterfront, several parties were going on aboard the big motor-yachts anchored in the marina, and in the background there was the steady hum of traffic driving along the main road. Michelle tried to tell herself that she wasn't worried, but as the hours dragged by and the day gave way to night, she had become increasingly anxious. What if something had happened to him? What if he'd had an accident?

When she finally saw him walking down the jetty she could have cried with relief. Springing to her feet, she ran to the side and grabbed his arm as soon as he came near, almost unbalancing him as he swung a leg over the rail.

'Where have you been?' she demanded in the fury that always follows relief. 'I expected you back hours ago!'

Guy's dark eyebrows rose in surprise. 'The chap I was seeing insisted on taking me out to dinner.' His tone sharpened. 'Why, what's happened?'

Michelle tried to get a grip on herself, guessing that he would hate anyone, especially a woman, to act possessively over him. 'Nothing. It's just—that I was—was worried about you,' she answered lamely, half turning away and looking down at her bare feet.

Guy was silent for a moment, then said gently, 'I'm sorry. I'm not used to anyone worrying about me, you see.'

That statement, and the tone in which it was said, made her head jerk up in surprise. But there was no time to read his expression because he was holding a large box out to her, a grin on his face.

'Here, isn't this what you've been waiting for?'

'What is it?'

'Clothes, of course.' And then he laughed as her face lit up with pleasure.

'Oh, Guy, *thank* you!' She made a grab at the box as he playfully raised his arm so that she had to jump for it. Her other hand she put on his shoulder, and finished up leaning against him. For a second her face was close to his. Without stopping to think about it, she kissed him quickly on the mouth, whispered huskily, 'I'm glad you're back,' then took the box from his hand and ran down below with it.

In her cabin she emptied the box on her bunk and went through the contents ecstatically. First there was a pair of pretty, colourful sandals that fitted perfectly and felt terribly strange after walking around in bare feet for so long. She tried a couple of turns round the cabin and discovered that she'd have to learn how to walk in high heels all over again. Next she found a pale blue cotton bikini, a pair of white shorts with a red and white striped sun-top to go with them, and also some underclothes: a couple of pairs of pants with matching bras. Michelle exclaimed with pleasure, tried everything on and couldn't fault a thing. All her life she had always had as many clothes as she wanted, but none of them had given her anything like the thrill that these did. She twisted in front of the mirror trying to see her back view, realising that Guy must have a great deal of experience at buying clothes for women if he could just walk into a shop and pick out the right style, colour and size so unerringly. That thought gave her pause for a moment, but she shrugged it off; she already knew that, didn't she?

There were some cosmetics in the box, lipstick, eye-shadow, mascara, etc., and one other garment, packed separately. It was a dress in soft, floating dark-gold silk. Carefully, Michelle removed it from its tissue wrappings and put it on. It was a young, simple style, sleeveless, with a fullish skirt and wide gold belt, but the shirt style top clung to her breasts and the belt emphasised the slimness of her waist. Slowly she picked up the cosmetics and began to apply them, then stepped back to look at herself critically. She looked what she was, a girl on the brink of womanhood. Her body had the firm tautness of youth, but there was femininity in the roundness of her breasts, the gracefulness of her neck and arms. Her tan helped, of course; the gold of the dress would have made her look pale and insipid without it, but now she looked like a creature of the sun, embraced by it and a part of it. Her hard work on the boat had made her lose weight and her face was thinner, emphasising the fine hollows of her cheeks, and her brown hair had a golden tint from the sun. She knew, with sudden certainty and excitement, that she had never looked better. She would never be beautiful, but she came very close to it now. She looked ready for life, for love.

Guy hadn't come down below or she would have heard him. With a little smile Michelle undid another button so that the soft swell of her breasts was revealed, and went up on deck to find him.

He was sitting on the squab seats on the afterdeck,

a drink in his hand and his legs stretched out in front of him. He had taken off his tie and his shirt was open at the neck, revealing a deep V of tanned skin. Michelle's heart jumped crazily and she had to take several deep breaths before she could walk out and stand in front of him.

'How do I look?' she demanded unevenly.

His eyes ran over her, but his face was in shadow and she couldn't tell what he was thinking. The sound of music drifted across to them from another boat, a soft, insidious love song.

At last he said, 'You look—very different.'

Just that, with nothing in his tone to tell her whether he approved or not.

Michelle laughed, trying to keep it light, and hoping that it didn't sound selfconscious. 'Well, I hoped I might.'

She hoped he might say something else too but, although his eyes were still on her, he seemed absorbed in something else, then he blinked and gave a quick shake of his head as if he was trying to pull himself together. 'Sorry. Would you like a drink?'

'No.' Michelle sat down beside him and leant back against the cushions. 'Thank you for the clothes.'

'I'm afraid I didn't have time to go to the Post Office today. I got those things from a shop in the hotel where we had dinner. But at least you'll have something to wear when you go shopping.'

'Yes.' Michelle slid along to lean against him.

'Cold?'

'A little.'

His arm lay on the back of her seat and he moved it forward so that it was across her shoulders. Michelle tucked her feet up under her and nestled against him.

'Is the broker going to look over the boat?'

'Mm. He seemed really interested. Said she sounds just the size that he could do with, and if she comes up to expectations he'll want to order several.' He had been idly running his fingers up and down her arm as he talked and Michelle could hardly keep from gasping aloud at the sensations his touch aroused in her.

'When is he coming?'

'Tomorrow morning. I'm not sure exactly when, but he said he'd try and make it as early as possible. I want to refuel and push on to Miami as soon as I can.'

He was silent for a while and Michelle knew a great feeling of contentment; to be held like this, even so casually, with his arm around her, close together in the soft darkness, with only the distant music and the soft lapping of the waves against the boat to disturb them. This was peace, this was heaven.

But presently his hand stopped, tightened a little, but his voice was quite offhand as he said, 'How about you? Will you stay in Bermuda for a while before you go back to England? You don't have to worry about money, by the way; I'll give you enough for your fare home and to keep you in Bermuda for a couple of weeks if you want to stay.'

'You don't have to give me any money . . .' Michelle began, but he cut in sharply.

'Nonsense! All boat crews have it written into their contract that they get their fare home. And besides, I owe you your wages.'

Taking her courage in both hands, Michelle said as lightly as she could, 'I'm enjoying the sun, but I don't think I particularly want to stay on in Bermuda. I think I'll go on to Miami with you.'

She felt him stiffen, then he straightened up in his

seat and took his arm from round her shoulders. 'Can't be done, I'm afraid,' he told her tersely. 'You have to have an entry visa to go to America.'

Michelle bit her lip, looking at the firm profile of his face in the moonlight, the straight nose, the strong, clean lines of his mouth and jaw. Somehow she had to try and break through that iron determination. 'That's no problem,' she told him. 'I could just stay on the boat, like I am now.'

'But I intend to sell the boat in Miami, not sail it back to London,' Guy said shortly. 'And anyway, you'd do better to go back to England.'

He moved to get up, but Michelle caught his arm. 'Please don't go. Not yet.'

Reluctantly he leant back again and she kept hold of his arm, feeling the hard muscles beneath the cloth of his jacket. Leaning her head on his shoulder again, she sought for the right words. 'It seems rather a waste to have at last got me working fairly efficiently and then to send me home before the voyage is over.'

'Why do you want to stay on?' he asked abruptly.

Because I love you, Michelle wanted to say, because just to see you, be near you, to touch you, makes my heart want to burst with happiness. But she couldn't say that, of course, not now, not yet, not ever perhaps. Emotion threatened to choke her and her voice was husky as she answered, 'Because I'm happy here on the *Ethos*. I'm happy with you,' she added daringly, and waited breathlessly for his reaction.

It was immediate rejection. Guy stood up and turned to face her, his features set into a hard mask. 'No, you're just happy because you're starting to grow up, to be free of some of your inhibitions at last. If you want to start experimenting with life then the sooner you get back to England the better.'

'I don't want to start experimenting,' Michelle returned tartly.

'Oh, yes, you do. Do you think I'm blind? I inadvertently roused your sexual curiosity those first few days aboard before I found out . . .' he paused, 'just how young you were. And now you can't wait to satisfy that curiosity.'

Michelle's hands curled into fists and she had to hide them in the folds of her skirt. Unsteadily she said, 'So don't you think you ought to finish—what you began?'

His jaw tightened. 'Why me? Why not one of your boy-friends back home?'

She licked lips gone suddenly dry. 'I've never known anyone like you before. My boy-friends, that's what they were—just boys, compared to you.'

Guy thrust his hands into his pockets and stared down at her in silence for what seemed an age, then he said shortly, 'So I happen to be the first older man you've ever been close to. But when you get home you'll probably meet someone, fall in love and be happy to give . . .'

'I won't!' Michelle interrupted forcefully, then, more gently, 'I know I won't. I want to stay here, with you.'

Guy's dark brows drew together into a frown. Brusquely he said, 'You're too young and inexperienced for me, Mitch. You're like a bud that's waiting to burst into flower.'

Slowly she stood up, a shaft of moonlight catching the soft folds of her dress and turning it to molten gold as she moved towards him. She stopped close by and gazed up at him. 'So—teach me,' she said softly, tentatively putting out her hand to touch his sleeve.

He didn't answer for a long moment, just stood staring down at her, then swung abruptly away until brought up short by the rail. Michelle's hand dropped limply to her side and she knew she'd lost even before he spoke.

'When I make love to a woman it's on equal terms,' he told her bluntly. 'That of teacher isn't my role. Go back home and do your experimenting with someone your own age, Mitch. I don't give lessons to little girls!' he added cruelly.

Desolation filled her heart, but somehow she managed to say with quiet dignity, 'Oh, but you do. Not in the way you mean, perhaps, but I've learnt a lot from you on this trip.' She shivered suddenly and put her hands up to rub her arms. 'It's chilly, and I'm rather tired. Goodnight, Guy.' She walked past him to the galley steps, then paused. 'Thank you again for the clothes. You have very good taste.'

He was watching her, a strangely intent look on his face, his hands still thrust into his pockets, and for a moment he didn't answer, then he merely said, 'Goodnight, Mitch,' and she nodded and went down the steps.

'Mitch! Mitch, where are you?'

Guy's voice reached to where Michelle was sitting on the swimming platform at the stern of the boat, dabbling her bare feet in the water and watching some windsurfers trying to stay upright behind their colourful sails farther along the bay.

'I'm here.' She got up, climbed the ladder on to the deck and ran towards him. He had gone into the town only a quarter of an hour ago and she hadn't expected him back so soon. 'It's all right, your broker friend didn't turn up while you were away.'

But he hardly seemed interested. His brows were

drawn into a frown and there was a grim look in his eyes as he said tersely, 'I've just been to the Post Office; your passport isn't there.'

'Oh.' Taken by surprise, Michelle could feel colour coming into her cheeks despite her efforts to control it. 'Isn't it?' she added lamely.

Guy's eyes had narrowed. 'No, it isn't—and I rather think you knew it wouldn't be there all along,' he bit out menacingly, taking a step towards her.

Michelle laughed nervously and backed away. 'But how could I?'

'I don't know, but I'm certainly going to find out.'

He made a lunge for her, but Michelle turned and fled, heading for the galley steps and the temporary safety of her cabin door between them. Temporary, she knew, because Guy wouldn't let it stand in his way for long. But she had only got half way down the deck before he caught her and swung her round.

'You knew that passport wasn't going to be there, didn't you? Didn't you?' he repeated, grabbing her other wrist and pushing her back against the main saloon bulkhead.

'Of course I didn't. Let me go, you're hurting my wrists!' Michelle knew that she'd given herself away, but she tried desperately for time to think.

But Guy didn't give her time for anything. He used his body to stop her struggles and demanded, 'I want the truth and I want it now. Who was the man whose address you gave me? Did he really have your passport?'

'Mind your own damn business! *Let me go!*' Fear made her raise her voice and continue to struggle, arching her back and trying to wrench her wrists free. She was wearing just the new bikini and Guy his shorts and a loose cotton sports shirt. As she struggled her legs rubbed against his and she could feel the hardness of his body pressing against her thighs. She began to pant with exertion, the moist gleam of sweat on her skin.

'You're going to tell me, you little bitch. D'you hear me? Or I'll . . .'

But whatever threat he was going to make was bitten off as a voice behind them with an American accent, drawled out, 'Hey there! Am I interrupting something?'

Guy swung his head round to look at the man who had climbed on to the deck, then slowly let her go. 'Nothing that can't wait,' he answered grimly as he gave Michelle a threatening look, his breath still rapid and uneven.

He moved forward to greet the man while Michelle rubbed her wrists, grateful for the breathing space but knowing that Guy would make her give him the answers he wanted as soon as they were alone again. The visitor was obviously the expected broker, but he seemed in no hurry to look over the boat, instead running his eyes over Michelle in a frank appraisal that brought a flush to her cheeks.

He turned to Guy. 'Have you got many more like her in the crew?' he asked with a grin that was close to a leer.

'No, just the one,' Guy returned evenly.

'Can't say I blame you, she looks hot enough for any man to handle.'

'How she looks is none of your damn business,' Guy snapped out, his brows drawn together into a frown.

The American held up his hands in a sign of peace. 'Okay! So it's like that. I'm sorry, I didn't realise.'

'Then let's get down to business, shall we?' Guy

said curtly, leading the man towards the stern.

Michelle went back to her seat on the swimming platform to wait until the man left. It took a long time; he spent over an hour going over every inch of the boat with Guy, and then they sat together in the main saloon for at least another hour; discussing terms presumably. Michelle hoped fervently that Guy would succeed in obtaining a favourable deal so that he would be in a good mood. She tried to think what she was going to do, how much to tell him, but everything had changed now; the wish to punish her parents had faded before her all-consuming determination to stay with Guy as long as she possibly could, no matter what she had to do to achieve it. But against this she felt a strong desire to tell him the truth, to have everything open and straight between them, to wipe the slate clean and not have to pretend any more. But if she did that, she had no doubt at all that he would immediately hand her over to the nearest Customs official and have her put on the first plane back to England. Michelle bit her lip and looked down at her feet, oddly distorted in the gently lapping water. Even when she saw the broker leave, she still hadn't made up her mind what to do.

She stood up and braced her shoulders, expecting Guy to come for her as soon as they were alone, but to her surprise he went back down below again. Nervously she walked towards the galley steps, her wet feet leaving footprints on the deck that dried almost immediately in the sun. At the doorway to the galley she hesitated, wondering whether or not to go down and confront him, expecting to see him reappear at any second.

But it was several minutes before he came into the galley and saw her hovering uncertainly in the doorway. His mouth was drawn into a thin, grim line and there was a cold, almost bleak look in his grey eyes. He stopped by the table, looking up at her, and Michelle felt herself go cold before the ice in his gaze.

'Come here,' he ordered abruptly.

Slowly she obeyed, having to force her legs into mobility. 'Guy, please don't be angry. I'm sorry if I deceived you, but I had to because I . . .' She started off in a rush, eager to see that look gone from his face, but her voice faded as his expression only grew grimmer.

'Oh, please go on,' he insisted with icy politeness. 'You were about to give me an explanation for all the lies you've told me, weren't you? It should make interesting listening.'

'What—what do you mean?'

'You know full well what I mean,' Guy bit out, his tone scathing. 'I doubt if one word you've said to me on this whole trip has been the truth. I've under-estimated you, you're not the young innocent that I thought. Are you, Miss June Mitchell—if that's your name?' Adding, when he saw her face flush with colour, 'No, I see it's not. That was just another of the lies, was it?'

'I'm sorry,' she began, feeling helpless before such sarcasm, but Guy interrupted her almost at once.

'Oh, please don't waste your time in apologising— we both know you don't mean it.' His voice changed, had a razorlike edge to it. 'So why don't you get down to telling me just who you are and why you stowed away on my boat?'

Michelle looked at him in dismay; she had expected him to be angry about her passport, but nothing like this. Falteringly she answered, 'But I didn't stow away. I *told* you, I fell in the river and drifted down to your boat. Then I fell asleep in the cabin.'

'And you really expect me to believe that?' he demanded scornfully.

'It's true. I swear it.'

'Really? And the address you gave me for your passport—was that true?'

Michelle lowered her head, licking her lips. 'No,' she replied in little more than a whisper. 'That wasn't true.'

'And your name—is it really June Mitchell?'

She shook her head, feeling about three inches tall and wishing she was anywhere but here, having to face the derision in his eyes.

'So what is your name?'

'Look,' Michelle said uncomfortably, 'let me try and tell you what happened. I *was* at a party and I *did* fall in the Thames, just like I said. Only I was—well, sort of running away from someone and . . .'

'Who?' Guy cut in abruptly.

'Who doesn't really matter. All that *does* matter is that I finished up on the *Ethos* and fell asleep in the cabin where you found me. At the time I was rather fed-up and—and unhappy about—certain people in my life, so I decided to teach them a lesson. That's why I asked you to take me with you; I wanted to disappear for a while to give them a fright, make them worry about me.'

'Oh, come now, surely you can make up a more convincing story than that?'

There was such utter disbelief and scorn in his tone that Michelle felt suddenly afraid, but she said with as much dignity as she could, 'I know I deceived you at first and I'm sorry, but I was upset and angry. I made up that story of being in France with a man because I didn't want you to know that

I'd been on board since London, and I invented an address to send to for my passport because I didn't want to give you my real name and address.'

'And that's the whole story, is it; that you were running away from someone and decided to teach them a lesson by coming to sea with me?' he asked more mildly.

'Yes,' Michelle assured him, glad that he seemed to be accepting it at last.

'You're quite sure you've missed nothing out?'

'Qu—quite sure,' she agreed with less certainty, wondering why he hadn't again demanded her real name.

His voice suddenly savage, Guy demanded, 'Then just what the hell were these doing hidden away in the drawer in your cabin?' And he put his hand in his pocket and pulled out the jewellery she had worn the night she ran away, scattering the pieces on the dark plastic surface of the galley table where the diamonds rolled and sparkled, catching the sunlight and reflecting it on a hundred different facets.

Michelle's first reaction was surprise because she'd forgotten all about them, then mounting indignation as she realised that he must have searched her cabin to find them.

She turned on him angrily. 'How dare you? You have no right to go through my things!'

'This is my boat and I'll go anywhere I damn well please,' Guy returned with equal heat. 'Now, just where did you get those and who do they belong to?'

'They're mine.'

He laughed in her face. 'What a great little actress you are, whatever your name is. But you've told just one lie too many.' Without warning he reached out and caught her wrist, twisting her arm up behind her back. 'There's only one way I'm going to get anything near the truth out of you, and that's by force. Now, where did you get them? Did you steal them? Are you on the run from the police? Is that why you hid on my boat?'

'No! It's not like you think. I told you they're mine. You swine, you're hurting me. Let me go!'

'Oh, no. Not till you've told me what I want to know.'

He jerked her arm up higher and Michelle cried out in pain. 'It's true, I tell you. They were presents.'

'Presents? Who from?' Mercifully he stopped pulling on her arm.

'From—from . . .' She tried to speak, but her voice was muffled by pain and sobs.

'Tell me,' he shouted at her. 'Were they from men?'

Hastily, afraid he would hurt her again, Michelle cried out, 'No! They were from my mother! And Peter.'

'Who's Peter?'

'He's my—he was my fiancé.'

Guy let her go so suddenly that she almost fell, then he spun her round to face him. 'You're engaged?'

Tremblingly Michelle nursed her injured wrist. 'I—I was. I'm not any more.'

'What do you mean?' he demanded, his voice so thunderous that she jumped. His face, too, was black, his brows drawn together and his jaw thrust forward in anger.

Michelle cringed inside, but she managed to say unsteadily, 'That night I fell in the river—I'd been to my engagement party—that's what the jewellery was for, you see.' Her finger came out to point at the ring. 'Peter gave me the ring and my mother gave me the rest. But—but . . .' she bit her lip as the memories came back, then went on wretchedly, 'but then Peter kept giving me a lot to drink, and he took me outside to his car. He wanted to make love to me, but I couldn't—not like that, but he'd had a lot to drink too and wouldn't stop when I said no. So I ran away from him and tried to hide, and that's when I fell in the river.'

Guy was silent for such a long time that she sneaked a look at him. He was staring at her, a white, set look to his face, but when he saw her looking at him, he frowned and said, 'Did anyone see you get on the *Ethos*?'

Dumbly she shook her head and Guy's voice sharpened.

'Are you saying that no one knows you're here? That as far as your parents, your fiancé knows, you could have drowned in the river?' he asked incredulously.

Michelle gulped, then nodded, knowing how angry he would be.

She was right; he straightened up and glared at her. 'You heartless little bitch! Don't you ever stop to think about other people's feelings?'

'I told you—I was unhappy. I wanted to teach them a lesson.' It sounded silly now, pathetic, but she had been so bitter and resentful at the time that it had seemed the natural thing to do.

'You let people who care about you think you're dead for nearly two weeks? My God, you're something else!'

Stung, Michelle retorted, 'I didn't know it would be this long. I thought it would only take a few days.'

Guy looked at her scornfully and the derision was

hard to take. She opened her mouth to try and explain why she'd done it, but then closed it again; he would never understand because he'd never had to experience anything like that. He turned and took a couple of impatient steps around the galley that always seemed too small to contain him.

Then he said curtly, 'Go and get your things together.'

She looked at him nervously. 'Why?'

'Because I'm going to hand you straight over to the authorities, that's why. They'll contact your people and see that you're sent home.'

'That won't be necessary. I've already written and told them that I'm okay.'

His eyes, cold and disbelieving, swung round to her face, 'How—and when?'

'Yesterday,' Michelle admitted. 'When you'd gone ashore. I wrote the letters and—gave them to a boy to post.'

'Well, I suppose that's something. Although you know perfectly well that it must take days for letters to reach England. What exactly did you tell them?'

'I told my parents that I was alive and well.'

'And your fiancé?'

Michelle licked lips gone suddenly dry. 'I told him that I didn't want to marry him any more.'

Guy's jaw came forward and he eyed her keenly. 'Did you tell any of them how you got here, that you were with me?'

She shook her head silently.

'Why not?'

'Because I don't want to go back. I want to stay with you.'

His face hardened. 'That's impossible and you know it. I'm taking you ashore right now so that your people can be informed immediately.'

'No, I won't go.'

She stood in trembling defiance as he took a menacing step towards her. 'What did you say?'

'I said I won't go—and I'm not going to tell you my name either!'

He glared at her furiously for a minute, then to her surprise, said, 'All right, don't,' adding sneeringly, 'Do you really think that not telling me is going to make any difference? Just how many girls do you think were reported missing in the Thames on that night? All I have to do is to radio back to England to find out who you are. I can have the information within an hour.' His left eyebrow rose disparagingly. 'Well, are you going to be sensible or do I use the radio?'

Michelle looked away, feeling the prick of tears behind her eyes. Reluctantly she answered, 'My name's—Michelle Bryant.'

It didn't mean anything to him. Coldly he went on, 'And your parents' address?'

She lifted her head to look at him, watching for his reaction. 'I told you, my parents are divorced. My father lives in America and I haven't seen him for a long time. My mother lives in London and will be too busy with her new play to do more than have her secretary send me a plane ticket home.'

Guy frowned at the bitterness in her voice. 'Just who are your parents?'

'My father is Sir Richard Bryant and my mother is Adele Verlaine. I see you've heard of them,' she added cynically as she saw his eyes widen in recognition.

'Who hasn't?' He stared down at her. 'My God, Mitch, what did they do to you to make you hate them like this?'

'I don't hate them, not really. I just wanted them

to *notice* me, to realise I was there, that's all,' she burst out. 'They were always so busy—with new plays, new films, new wives, new lovers. And because I couldn't act and wasn't beautiful like my mother they had no time for me. I was just in the way.' She reached out and caught hold of his shirt, looked up at him pleadingly. 'Oh, please, Guy, can't you see? Can't you understand?'

His hands came up to cover hers, held them still as he looked down at her searchingly. 'Maybe I can,' he said at length. 'But you must see that it doesn't make any difference. I can't take you with me. I have to hand you over to the Bermudan authorities today.'

'No!' She threw herself against him. 'I won't go!'

'Mitch, there's no other way.' He tried to push her away, but immediately he did so she put her arms round his waist and clung tightly.

'Please don't make me go back!' She raised her head and looked at him, her eyes wet with tears. Tremblingly, her eyes searching his face, she said, 'I—I love you. Please don't send me away.'

For a brief second she thought she saw some sort of reaction in his face, but then it set into a hard mask and he wrenched her arms free and pushed her forcefully away. 'No, you don't.'

'It's true!' Anxiously she tried to convince him, but he rounded on her fiercely.

'Is it? Or is it just another one of your lies? Okay,' he cut in as she was about to interrupt, 'maybe you think you are in love with me, but last month you thought you were enough in love with someone else to get engaged to him. And maybe next month you'll have fallen for another man and will have forgotten that I ever existed.'

'No.' Michelle shook her head helplessly, knowing

that he didn't even want to believe her. A tear of humiliation ran down her cheek and she put up a hand to knuckle it away like a child.

Guy turned to stare out of the window. His voice gratingly harsh, he said, 'Go and get your things together; I'm taking you ashore.'

'No.'

There was almost a tired note in Guy's voice as he said, 'It's no use fighting me, Mitch. You're going ashore if I have to carry you.'

'No, I won't go and you can't make me.' Raising her chin defiantly as he turned angrily to face her, Michelle played her last card. 'Because if you do I'll tell everyone that you kept me on your boat by force and that you . . .' for a moment her courage almost failed her as she saw the growing menace in his eyes, but then she drew a long breath and went on determinedly, 'and I'll tell them that you molested me.'

CHAPTER EIGHT

FOR a moment there was a shattering silence before Guy said, 'Are you trying to threaten me?'

'Yes,' Michelle agreed, 'I think I am.'

'And do you really think anyone is going to believe you?' he demanded incredulously.

'Why shouldn't they? After all, it's partly true,' she reminded him, gathering her courage. 'You did try to—to make love to me.'

He looked at her scornfully. 'You're wasting your time. Nothing you can say is going to stop me handing you over.'

'Not even the fact that I'll give a press interview and tell the whole world that you abducted me? You don't really think that anyone will buy any of your boats then, do you, Guy? That's if they don't arrest you and put you in prison, that is.'

A flame of anger lit the grey eyes. 'You know, Mitch,' he told her viciously, 'you're really a dirty fighter. When you want something you don't care how many lies you tell or who you hurt so long as you get your own way, do you?'

She flushed, shook her head, then said, 'I'm sorry. I just want to be with you.'

He looked at her coldly for a long moment, then seemed to make up his mind. 'All right, you can stay on board.'

'And you promise not to tell the authorities I'm here?'

Scornfully he agreed, 'No, I won't tell them.' Then, his tone changing abruptly, he went on,

'We've wasted enough time. Go and stand by to untie the mooring ropes, I want to take her over to the water point to refill the tanks.'

'You're leaving for Miami today?' Michelle asked him, glad that there was something impersonal to talk about, something practical to do.

'No, the broker is going to draw up a contract for me to sign, and then there's the import licence from this end and the export licence from England to be seen to. Also I want to check the engines over after we've filled up with fuel and water.'

'But we'll be leaving soon?' Michelle asked anxiously, thinking of the letters she'd written.

'Just as soon as I can make it. I don't want to stay here any longer than you do.'

But two days later he was still waiting to sign the contracts. He was told there was a delay in obtaining the import licence because the office had closed for the weekend and he would have to wait until Monday. During those two days Guy was completely unapproachable. He seemed to have placed a steel barrier between them that she couldn't penetrate. He didn't talk to her much except to give orders and when he wasn't busy on the engines or some other part of the boat, he sat on deck in the sun and fished, or read a book. When he did look at her his eyes were cold, implacable, and Michelle knew that he deeply resented the way she had blackmailed him into letting her stay. She too was wretched and miserable, knowing that she'd made the greatest mistake of her life in telling him that she loved him, that he didn't care for her and now probably never would.

Only once did they have a real conversation. They were sitting across the dinner table from one another when, at the end of the meal, Guy broke the long, uncomfortable silence by asking abruptly, 'Your fiancé—how long have you known him?'

Michelle looked up in surprise. 'Peter? Just over a year.'

'How old is he?'

'Twenty-two.'

'And what does he do?'

'He works in his father's stockbroking firm,' she answered uneasily, wondering where all these questions were leading.

'He sounds extremely respectable,' Guy commented drily.

'Yes, he is.'

He leaned forward, said persuasively, 'Look, Mitch, I know you said he went too far and frightened you at your party, but I'm sure that if you saw him again you'd soon make it up.'

'No, I wouldn't,' Michelle answered positively. 'Because I was never in love with him.'

'But you must have thought you were to get engaged.'

'No.'

'Then just why did you get engaged to him?' Guy demanded on an exasperated note.

'Because he's middling.'

His eyebrows rose incredulously. 'Did you say middling?'

'Yes. He's middling good-looking, middling clever, middling rich, middle-class; just middling everything.'

'I suppose you had a reason for finding his talent for mediocrity so attractive,' Guy remarked, his tone heavy with sarcasm.

Michelle flushed, but answered steadily. 'My mother is very flamboyant, she's a creature of moods, especially in private, either on top of the world or depressed. And she's always going abroad or is away on tour somewhere. And then there are her lovers; I always have to keep out of the way when they're around because she doesn't like them to know she has a grown-up daughter. And besides,' she added cynically, 'I make her realise how old she is.' She paused, then went on, 'I suppose I got engaged to Peter just because he was so ordinary and so—so dull.'

Guy's mouth drew into a grim line. 'And you think you would have been happy with him?'

She lifted her head to look at him. 'I might have been—if I hadn't met you.'

A remark that brought the conversation to an abrupt end as Guy got up and walked out of the galley.

On Sunday they were woken by the Cathedral bells ringing out across the harbour, and the sound filled Michelle with a feeling of peace and contentment which was dispelled as soon as she saw Guy. He seemed extra terse and abrupt with her this morning, going on deck to do some odd jobs immediately after breakfast and staying up there. She watched him go, feeling wretched but determined to stick to her guns; if his attitude was meant to break her down then he would be disappointed, because she was certain that the only chance she had was to stay with him just as long as she could.

Dispiritedly she started washing up and was soon sunk in a reverie of what could be, what might have been if she hadn't resisted him at first, but presently her thoughts came back to here and now when her attention was caught by several large, gleaming limousines that drove fast up the main road and stopped at the end of the jetty, near the Customs shed. A woman and several men got out of the cars, including some in official-looking uniforms, and they began to hurry along the jetty. Then another couple of cars pulled up and half a dozen people carrying cameras jumped out and rushed after the others. Their attention was on a tall, dark-haired man wearing sunglasses who seemed to be heading the procession and the woman beside him who was mostly hidden by the taller men around her, the uniformed men clearing the way for them through the Sunday crowds of people. They were all hurrying along and Michelle watched them curiously, wondering who they were, but then they turned off the main jetty and started up the pier between the moored boats in the marina and she got a better look at the man and woman in the lead. The plate she was holding dropped from her hands back into the water as she stared. She ought to have known who it was at once, because the man's distinguished, handsome features were known to millions all over the world and the woman's still beautiful face was equally, if not better known. Anyone would know Sir Richard Bryant or Adele Verlaine when they saw them!

For a moment Michelle stood in utter confusion, wondering how on earth they had found out where she was. But there was only one way they could have known, only one person who could have told them. She ran out of the galley and along the deck, too furious to care that the photographers might see her.

Guy was standing in the bow, his hands on his hips, watching the crowd of people making their way towards the boat. There was a grim look on his face that swiftly changed as he heard her running footsteps.

'You told them! You pig! You promised you wouldn't!' Her face contorted by rage and mortification, Michelle tried to lash out at him, but Guy caught her arms and forced them down. Tears of frustrated anger came to her eyes as she vainly strained to break free of his grip. 'You promised,' she yelled at him. 'Oh, why did you do it? Do you hate me that much?'

His fingers bit hard into her flesh, hurting her suddenly. 'No,' he answered fiercely. 'Of course I don't hate you.'

'Then why did you do it? Why?'

'I *had* to let your parents know you were alive. To have left them in ignorance a moment longer than necessary would only have condoned what you've done, and I'm not that cruel, Mitch. But I kept my promise, I didn't tell the authorities here. Instead I radioed to England and told them to get in touch with your mother. I left it up to her whether she came for you or not.'

'Oh, she'd come all right. But you don't think it's me she cares about, do you? She just couldn't bear to pass up a chance for all this free publicity, that's all.'

'Mitch, that isn't true. She's probably worried sick . . .'

'Look at them,' Michelle broke in angrily on his attempt at reassurance. 'Don't you see the photographers? How the hell do you think they knew? Because she told them, of course. They're actors, Guy. They live by publicity, they thrive on it, my mother especially. Oh, why did you have to do it?'

He looked down at her face, at the tears on her cheeks, and the grim look came back to his mouth. 'Go on down to your cabin and clean yourself up,' he ordered. 'I'll stall them till you're ready.'

He pushed her ahead of him along the deck, making her obey him, and Michelle went unresistingly, knowing that it was all over, that her fight for love was lost before it had even begun. The people were only about a hundred yards away now and she heard someone give a shout of recognition as she moved to descend the galley steps, but she didn't look back, just ran ahead of Guy down into the bathroom and locked the door. Behind her she heard Guy shut the door leading from the galley to the cabins, and she quickly closed the window and curtains in the bathroom, afraid that some photographer would poke his camera through.

Slowly, miserably, she began to wash her face, trying to hide all trace of tears. The boat rocked as the people swarmed on board and there was the rise and fall of excited voices. She couldn't make out much except once when she heard Guy's raised voice saying sharply, 'Did you have to bring this circus with you?' Someone moved along the deck and tried the window and she started back in fear, but then they moved away again and she began to comb her hair, then pulled it back off her head and did it in a long plait which hung heavy on her back. She was barefoot, as usual, and had on the shorts and suntop that Guy had bought her. Her skin was tanned golden brown, but her face was very pale now beneath it. She wore no make-up, and that, plus the pigtail, made her look even younger than nineteen, but the sadness and loss that darkened her eyes was far beyond her years.

She waited for what seemed a long time. The boat rocked again a couple of times, but she didn't dare to draw the curtain to look out. At length she heard someone come out of the galley and then there was a rap on the door.

'Okay, Mitch, you can come out now.'

Hand shaking, she unlocked the door. Eagerly her

eyes went to Guy's face, but his features were set
into a hard, enigmatic mask. He motioned her ahead
of him into the galley and up the steps into the main
saloon, and she obeyed him numbly.

She had expected the boat to be thronged with
people, but to her surprise there were only four
others in the saloon, all of whom turned towards her
expectantly as she walked in.

'Darling!' Immediately her mother crossed to her
and put her arms round her, holding her close and
kissing her cheek. 'Oh, my poor darling! We thought
. . . oh, we thought something terrible had happened
to you!' Adele Verlaine moved back a little, tears in
her eyes as she searched Michelle's face.

'Hallo, Mother,' Michelle said woodenly, her nostrils full of the expensive perfume Adele Verlaine
always wore. She looked over her shoulder to where
her father stood and he gave her the lazy smile that
had won him three wives, a good many mistresses
and untold millions of fans. 'Hallo, Daddy.'

'Hallo, child. Welcome back to the land of the
living. You did have us feeling just a mite worried,
you know.'

'Worried!' her mother put in. 'I was out of my
mind!' She put up a hand to stroke Michelle's face,
but then said, 'But I'm being selfish. Look, darling,
here's Peter.'

Michelle turned her head to where Peter was
hovering in the background, waiting for someone to
notice him. He didn't get much chance with two
experienced actors upstaging him like mad. He came
towards her and put his hands on her shoulders, went
to kiss her, but Michelle turned her head away and
he ended up giving her a selfconscious peck on the
cheek, aware of everyone watching him.

'Hallo, Peter,' Michelle greeted him tonelessly.

He looked at her uncertainly, started to say, 'Darling, I . . .' but then his voice trailed off before the set expression on her face.

The fourth person in the room came forward into the sudden, uncomfortable silence. He wasn't wearing a uniform, but it was obvious that he was some sort of official.

'Miss Bryant, I'm sorry to bother you at such an emotional moment, but a good deal of time has been expended on looking for you and I need to know how you came to be aboard this boat.' His words were very polite, but there was a blunt, no-nonsense look about him that hinted at steel beneath his unprepossessing exterior.

Her voice flat and devoid of any emotion, Michelle explained how she'd fallen in the Thames, been carried to the boat and gone to sleep in the cabin, not waking until it was out to sea.

'I see.' The man made some notes on a pad. 'Were you aware, Miss Bryant, that this boat contains a radio powerful enough to transmit to England?'

'Yes.'

'And did you know that no radio message informing your parents that you were alive was sent until the early hours of yesterday morning?'

The early hours of the morning? So Guy must have waited to use the radio until she was asleep. She turned her head to look at him and found that he was leaning against the bulkhead, arms folded, watching her intently, his mouth set into a thin line.

'Miss Bryant?'

Slowly she turned to look back at the policeman, or whatever he was. 'Yes, I knew.'

'Was this by your wish, Miss Bryant, or did Mr Farringdon here refuse to pass on a message?'

She paused before answering and saw Guy stiffen,

although his features didn't alter. If she was going to
carry out her threat to accuse him now was the time.
Lifting up her head, she looked straight into his eyes
and said clearly, 'It was by my wish. I gave Mr
Farringdon a false name when he found me. He had
no idea who I was until Friday.'

Guy's eyes widened, he straightened up and his
arms came down to his sides.

But the man was going on, 'I must further ask
you, Miss Bryant, whether you have been molested
in any way or whether anything has been done to
you against your will?'

'No,' Michelle answered in little more than a
whisper. 'Nothing has been done to me, either
against my will or with it.'

She turned away then, her heart heavy with bitter
self-irony. The man was going on, saying something
about irresponsibility and waste of time, but she
didn't hear him, she was looking blindly out of the
window, aware only of the brilliant radiance of the
sun on the surface of the water. But then her father
cut the man short and he went away.

There was a long silence and she knew that they
were all looking at her, waiting for some kind of
explanation, but she just stood numbly looking out
of the window, unable to say a word.

At length Richard Bryant turned to Guy and held
out his hand. 'I think I owe you an apology, Mr
Farringdon. When we first heard that Michelle was
with you—well, you can imagine what we thought.
But now it seems I have to thank you for taking care
of her and to express our regret that you became
involved in our,' he hesitated, smiling ruefully, 'our
domestic difficulties. I trust,' he added, 'that we can
count on your discretion?'

Guy returned his look sardonically and made no

move to shake his hand. '*My* discretion? When you've brought that pack of press hounds with you?'

Her father shook his head. 'We didn't bring them, Farringdon; your radio message was intercepted by a radio ham and passed on to the press. Believe me, there's no one more sorry than I am; I would have kept this quiet if I could—Michelle's had enough to put up with, being our daughter, without this. And,' he went on, turning towards her, 'it seems that we still have quite a few problems to straighten out.'

'Yes, and I think we can best do that back at the hotel,' her mother put in. 'Darling, do you have any shoes?'

'Yes, I'll get them,' Michelle answered dully, and left them while she went to her cabin to get her things. She moved lethargically at first, looking round the little cabin, knowing it would be for the last time, and remembering, but then she had a sudden revulsion of feeling and began to cram the clothes in a bag and throw the jewellery in after them. Cosmetics, diamonds, comb, they all went in anyhow. Scrabbling her hand in the drawer, she found an earring at the very back and went to pull it out, but then her hand paused and she pushed it back again. Maybe it was a forlorn hope, maybe he wouldn't find it, or if he did would just send it to her, but it was a chance of seeing him again, even if a very slim one.

A silence fell as she strode into the saloon, the sort of sharp silence when people have been caught talking about you, but Michelle merely said, 'I'm ready,' and made for the door.

'Michelle!' Her father's sharp command stopped her in the doorway. 'I believe you have something to say to Mr Farringdon before we leave.'

Michelle's eyes closed tightly for a moment, then

her shoulders came up and she turned to face them all. Going over to Guy, she kept her eyes on a level with his chest and said in a polite, little-girl voice, 'Thank you for letting me stay on your boat, Mr Farringdon, and I'm sorry if I've caused you any inconvenience.' Then she immediately turned and walked out of the saloon with her parents hurrying after her.

The *papparazzi* were waiting at the end of the pier, held back by several policemen, and there was also a growling crowd of grinning onlookers, excited that their Sunday strolls had brought them for a moment close to something of newsworthy importance. Her parents did their best to shield her, walking on either side of her and hurrying along to the car, Peter bringing up the rear. For a few minutes it was hell, with flashlights going off close to her face and questions being shouted at her, but then they were in the limousine and racing away from the harbour. Michelle didn't turn to look back, she kept her eyes down until they had arrived at a hotel, passed the curious eyes in the foyer and were safely in the two-bedroom suite her mother had taken on the second floor.

'Now,' her father said as soon as they were inside, 'you've got some explaining to do, young lady.'

Michelle looked at them, then fished in her bag for the engagement ring. Holding it in the palm of her hand, she crossed to Peter. 'I want to give this back to you. I'd already written to you to tell you I was breaking off the engagement. You'll probably find the letter waiting for you when you get home.'

He looked at her in shocked amazement. 'But why? Surely you don't . . .'

'I think you know why,' she interrupted brusquely.

He flushed and looked away, then said desperately, 'Look, Michelle, we both had a lot to drink that night and it wasn't my fault you . . .' But then he saw the scorn in her eyes and stopped, biting his lip. Reluctantly he reached up and took the ring from her hand, looking down at it miserably.

'Thank you. I'm sorry your journey here was a waste of time.'

Michelle turned away and Peter stood looking around at them rather helplessly until Richard Bryant took him by the arm and led him outside.

As the door closed behind them her mother said, 'That was extremely cruel.'

'Yes,' Michelle agreed bitterly, 'but then I've had plenty of opportunity to learn how to be cruel, haven't I? And anyway,' she added with ironical insight, 'he'll soon get over it. He was more in love with the fact that I was your daughter than he was with me.'

They were silent then until Richard Bryant came back a few minutes later. 'He's going back to England on the next plane,' he told them. He looked at Michelle keenly. 'Do you want to tell us what happened on the night of your engagement party? And why you didn't let us know you were alive?' he added heavily.

Michelle shrugged. 'It really doesn't matter now, does it? I was unhappy and there didn't seem to be anything to go back to, so I stayed away. I'm sorry if you were upset at all, but I didn't think you'd care much one way or the other.'

There was a sharp silence before Richard Bryant turned furiously on her mother. 'You bitch! What the hell have you done to her? I should never have let you keep her. I should have insisted on taking her to America with me when we split up, as I wanted to do.'

Adele Verlaine's lovely face was pale beneath the make-up. 'Richard, I swear to you, I . . .'

'Don't bother,' he cut in scornfully. 'I've heard all your excuses and promises a thousand times before.' He turned to Michelle. 'I'm sorry, darling, I thought you were happy. I thought . . . Well, okay, I took the easy way out and presumed you were happy. But it seems I was wrong all along. You're coming back to the States to live with me. You won't have to stay with your mother any longer.'

'No,' Michelle said decisively. 'I'm going back to England. And when I get there I'll find a job and a place of my own. I don't need either of you any longer. I don't need . . .' her voice broke for a second but was quickly covered, 'I don't need anyone.'

She went to her own room then, only coming out to join them for lunch, which was eaten mostly in a tense silence. That her parents had been discussing her, she knew, but didn't much care; which was ironical when she remembered that her reason for going with Guy had been precisely to achieve this end: getting them together and taking some notice of her. The phone rang several times, but they were all media enquiries, wanting them to give an interview. Some people managed to get as far as the door, too, and Michelle would stiffen with anticipation every time there was a knock, but it was never Guy, and she began to give up hope.

But at six-thirty, when she was changing for dinner, her mother's maid knocked on the bathroom door and told her that Mr Farringdon was downstairs.

'Oh, yes, ask him to come up, would you. I won't be a minute.'

Breathlessly Michelle dried herself, wishing that

she'd been ready, that he'd come at any other time than this, desperately hoping that she could find some way to get through to him. She put on her underclothes and then a sumptuously luxurious long white bathrobe of her mother's that was hanging behind the door. Her hand trembled as she brushed her hair and she would have liked to put on some make-up. But there was no time, he might just leave the earring and go.

But even though she was in such a desperate hurry, she paused with her hand on the door of the sitting-room, suddenly afraid. But then she pushed it open, her eyes going eagerly to Guy as soon as she entered the room. He was standing with his back to her, looking out of the window which overlooked the gardens at the front of the hotel. He was wearing another of his business suits, a navy one this time. When he heard the door open he turned slowly to look at her. He didn't smile or attempt to greet her, just stood looking at her, his face a stern, hard mask.

Her voice dry in her throat, Michelle took refuge in social good manners. 'Good evening. Can I get you a drink?'

For a moment he continued to look at her, then nodded. 'Thank you. I'll have a Scotch and soda.'

Michelle went to the drinks tray and poured it for him, her trembling hands spilling some of the amber liquid. 'Would you like ice?'

'No, thanks.'

She crossed to give it to him, looking into his eyes and then quickly away again as their coldness struck her.

'I found this in your cabin after you'd gone.' He put his hand into his pocket and pulled out the earring, holding it out to her. It reminded her forcefully of how she'd held out the engagement ring to Peter;

but somehow she couldn't believe that he had felt even half the reluctance she felt as she reached out to take it.

Her eyes searched Guy's face, but he raised his glass and drank from it before saying abruptly, 'Why didn't you accuse me of abducting you as you threatened?'

'I don't know.' Michelle turned and walked a little away from him. 'Because I couldn't when it came to it, I suppose.'

'Well, I'm grateful, for what it's worth; it will enable me to get away tomorrow.'

'You're leaving tomorrow?'

'Yes.' He drained his glass in one swallow and put it down. 'I'd better be going. Goodbye, Mitch.'

'No! Don't go. I . . .' She moved between him and the door, looked up at him pleadingly. 'Guy, I meant what I said back there on the boat. I want to go with you.'

'Did you leave your earring behind on purpose?' he demanded.

'Yes. I wanted to see you again. I—I love you, Guy.'

His jaw tightened. 'So you said before. But you just think you do, that's all. You said yourself that I'm different from all the men you've known. It was being thrown together with an older man, someone who treated you like a grown woman and not a child, that made you feel like this.'

'That isn't true! I *know* how I feel. Nothing will make me change.' She caught hold of his sleeves, gazing up at him beseechingly. 'Please believe me. I . . .'

'No!' He caught her wrists and pulled them down. 'You're no more in love with me than I am with you.'

That hurt, and Michelle flinched as if he'd struck her, but she said steadily, 'I don't believe you. I think you do care for me. Oh, it may not be very much, not enough to call—to call love, but I think you do care for me a little.'

Angrily he turned his back on her. 'You're mistaken,' he retorted harshly.

Michelle's chest heaved as she struggled to keep control of her emotions. 'You know, Guy,' she said chokily, 'I feel sorry for you. Just because a woman hurt you once you're afraid to even admit to your own feelings, let alone show any emotion. You're just afraid to let yourself fall in love!'

Guy stared at her, his face white around his set mouth, a savagely angry light in his eyes. He took a hasty step towards her, but stopped precipitately as he heard a door open and her mother came into the room.

'Why, Mr Farringdon, how nice to see you again. I'm sorry I wasn't here to greet you, but I was changing for dinner.'

Guy recovered himself superbly, there wasn't a trace of anger left in his face as he moved forward to shake hands. He smiled warmly, his eyes running over Adele Verlaine's perfect figure in a long, swathed black dress with a plunging neckline. 'It was well worth the wait,' he told her appreciatively.

Adele smiled at him, her eyes assessing him as a man. 'How different you look tonight, Mr Farringdon—or may I call you Guy?'

'By all means.' Adele sat down on a sofa and looked at him invitingly. Immediately he crossed to sit beside her, giving her all his attention.

Michelle turned away, feeling sick inside. Was this to be the final degradation? That the man she loved should become just another of the men who fawned at her mother's feet, overwhelmed by her beauty and charm?

'Darling, why don't you pour us out some drinks, and then I really think you ought to get dressed, don't you? You can borrow something of mine, if you like,' Adele added, as if she was giving her a treat.

Somehow Michelle poured the drinks and took them over. Guy hardly bothered to glance up before turning back to smile and laugh at something her mother was saying as she exerted her charm to attract him. Stiffly she went back to her bedroom to finish dressing. When she came back they'd gone, and the maid told her that they had gone out to dinner together.

'Your mother said that she thought you'd prefer to have dinner alone with Sir Richard,' the maid told her with unwanted sympathy in her tone.

It was very late before they got back. Michelle was lying in bed and heard the door open and her mother's voice followed by Guy's laugh. The voices continued for a little while and she lay there rigidly, hating them both, waiting to hear them go into her mother's bedroom, but instead she heard the sound of the outer door closing. Her eyes flew wide open as she stared into the darkness, hardly able to believe her ears. Quickly she got up and went to the door to listen. There was only the sound of her mother's footsteps as she went to her room. Bewildered, Michelle went to the window in the hope that she might see Guy as he left the hotel. He came out of the entrance a few minutes later and paused on the steps to light a cigarette. The doorman approached him and gestured towards a waiting taxi, but Guy shook his head and began to walk through the gardens. He went slowly, as if he was preoccupied, and he paused when he was almost opposite and looked up at the windows of the suite.

Michelle's room was in darkness and she knew he couldn't see her, but even so she drew back, afraid of being seen. Guy continued to gaze up for a while longer, then he turned and sat on a low stone wall while he finished his cigarette. There was a hibiscus bush growing nearby, the pale lemon-coloured flowers looking ghostlike in the moonlight. As Michelle watched, Guy reached out and plucked one of the blooms and held it in his hand. It was just a bud, its petals folded tightly over one another; waiting for the morning and the sun that would give it the light and warmth it needed to open its petals and display its vivid beauty. Guy ran his finger along it, stroking it gently, and Michelle suddenly remembered a phrase he had once used: 'You're like a bud waiting to burst into flower.'

A strange, tense excitement gripped her as she watched, and she was hardly aware that her mother had come into the room until she was by her side, her hand on Michelle's shoulder. Following her daughter's gaze, she, too, saw Guy in the garden. Michelle expected her to make some remark, but never the one she did.

'Are you very much in love with him?'

Slowly Michelle turned to face her mother. For a second she thought of denying it, but then her chin came up and she answered, 'Yes, I am.'

'So why don't you tell him so?' Adele Verlaine asked mildly.

'I already have. He doesn't want me. You should know that,' Michelle added bitterly.

'Should I? How?'

'Well, it was you he took out tonight.'

'Yes. But not because he wanted to.'

'What do you mean? He was obviously attracted to you.'

'Rather too obviously, I think. Oh, good heavens, Michelle, do you think I can't tell the difference between genuine feelings and acting by now? He couldn't have cared less about me. Once we were outside the door he was merely politely charming. He was just using me.'

'B-but why? I don't understand.'

'Because he thought that taking me out and showing me attention would finally put you off him, of course.'

'He was right, it did,' Michelle answered shortly.

'Then you're as big a fool as he is.'

'He isn't a fool,' she retorted, jumping swiftly to his defence.

'Yes, he is. All men in love are fools. He thinks he's all wrong for you and that you're just infatuated. And if you want him you're just going to have to convince him that it's for keeps.'

Michelle looked at her mother helplessly. 'But how? He won't listen to me.'

Impatiently her mother answered. 'Go after him, of course. Now. Before it's too late. Show him that you care. *Make* him take you with him.' Then she laughed at Michelle's amazed face. 'Well, don't just stand there, get dressed!'

Michelle took another look into the garden and saw Guy get up, grind his cigarette end into the earth and look down at the bud in his hand. His fingers closed over it and he looked as if he was going to throw it aside, but instead he thrust it deep into his jacket pocket before turning and striding quickly away.

Immediately she began to dress while her mother helped her.

'You can have one of my cases and I'll put some of my things in for you. Oh, and I brought your passport with me—you'll need that. And some toiletries, of course.'

She ran out of the room and returned with a partly filled suitcase into which she hastily put Michelle's own clothes. 'There, I think that's everything. Here's some money for a taxi, and in case you need it.'

'Thanks.' Michelle fastened the strap of her sandal and stood up to take the case. 'You'll say goodbye to Daddy for me, won't you, if I—if I don't come back?'

'Yes, of course.'

They hurried together to the outer door, but then Michelle paused uncertainly and turned to look at her mother searchingly. 'Why are you doing this for me?'

Adele Verlaine hesitated, then said, 'When your father and I were splitting up you still had his love, his unreserved, unbounded love, but I was losing it. He wanted to take you with him, but I wouldn't let him because I wanted to hurt him. And I was so jealous of you that I wouldn't even let you go and visit him when he wanted.' She looked down at her hands. 'Jealousy is a most terrible emotion, Michelle, it makes people do crazy things. But now perhaps I can make it up to you a little.' She leant forward and kissed her daughter. 'Good luck, my dearest. I hope you get the man you love, and once you've got him make sure you don't lose him like I did.' Lifting a hand, she touched Michelle's cheek and smiled at her mistily. 'Go now.'

But still Michelle hesitated. 'But what about you?'

'Me?' Adele Verlaine smiled. 'Well, your father's room is just down the corridor, and I've heard rumours that all isn't well between him and his current wife. So perhaps it may not be too late after all, and I'll go along there and see if I can't win back the man *I* love!'

They smiled at each other, both with a common bond that for the first time bridged their relationship, then Michelle turned and ran down the corridor to the lifts.

She took a taxi from the hotel, expecting to overtake Guy as he walked along, but the taxi cut through the town instead of going along the waterfront and she didn't see him. The boat was in darkness when she climbed aboard and she had to scramble through a window because the cabin door was locked. Once inside she hesitated, wondering what to do, but then she smiled and made her way to the main cabin, switching on the light to reveal the big circular bed. Swiftly she made it up with the specially fitted sheets that were kept in one of the drawers, listening all the time for the sound of Guy's footsteps. But she had time to hide her suitcase in a cupboard, to brush her long hair and put on a little make-up, and, after a long moment's hesitation, to take off all her clothes and put them away. Then she turned off the main light so that only the dim glow of the bedside lamps illuminated the cabin, that and the shafts of moonlight that came through the windows after she'd opened the curtains so that Guy would be sure to see the lights when he came aboard. One last look round and then she slid between the cool sheets to wait.

It was almost twenty minutes later before he arrived. Twenty minutes of rapidly growing tension and nervousness. His footsteps came quite slowly along the pier, hesitated near the boat as Michelle imagined him looking up and seeing the light, and then came on swiftly, purposefully. She sat up in the bed and pulled the sheets up to cover herself, her heart beating wildly.

The door burst open and then Guy stopped dead on the threshold, staring at her in total disbelief. Michelle had carefully worked out what she was going to say while she was waiting, but now every word of it had gone and she could only sit there like a fool and wait to see what he would do. It took him several seconds to recover, but then he came into the cabin and pushed the door shut.

'How long have you been here?'

'Not long. I took a taxi from the hotel shortly after you left.'

'I see.' His mouth set into a grim line. 'Well, you can just get dressed, because I'm taking you straight back.'

'I'm afraid I can't do that,' Michelle answered steadily enough. 'You see, I thought you'd try that one, so I threw all my clothes out of the window into the sea.'

'Did you, by God?' He moved towards the bed and stood looking down at her. 'I suppose you've run away again without letting your parents know where you are?'

'No. As a matter of fact my mother told me to come here. She seemed to think that you did care for me after all.'

'Indeed?' He was at his most disdainful.

'Yes,' Michelle persisted. 'And I think so too. If you look in your right-hand pocket you'll see why.'

Guy's eyebrows rose. He put his hand in his pocket and then his expression changed. He pulled out the hibiscus bud and looked down at it lying pale gold on his palm. Slowly he lifted his eyes to look at her.

'I remembered, you see, what you said, and it

gave me the courage to—to come here.' Her voice trailed off as he continued to stand and look at her so silently. Biting her lip, she looked down at the coverlet, began to pleat it nervously between her fingers, convinced that he was finding the words to send her away again. Perhaps the bud hadn't reminded him of her at all, perhaps it was someone else.

She was on the verge of breaking down into tears when he said almost conversationally, 'I knew that I was in love with you the day I helped you to catch a fish and then you cried because I killed it. I'd begun to suspect it before, but that was when I knew for certain.'

Michelle's head came up and she stared at him open-mouthed. He glanced at her and began to take off his jacket, throwing it on to a seat. Then he took off his tie. 'I told myself that I was thirteen years older than you and that you were too young to know your own mind, but it didn't make any difference.'

His shirt followed his tie on to the seat, then he sat on the bed to take off his shoes. Matter-of-factly he went on, 'Every time I saw you, touched you, I wanted you. Trying to act like some sort of older brother to you was pure hell, especially when you tried to provoke me like you did. The only way I could keep my hands off you was by telling myself that we'd soon be in Bermuda and you'd be leaving the boat.'

He slipped off his trousers, then turned to look at her fully for the first time. 'But then you told me all in one breath that you loved me but were engaged to someone else. I reckoned that the only decent thing I could do was to get the hell out of your life and if making you hate me by going out with your mother helped, then I'd do that too. But it seems it didn't work.'

'No,' Michelle agreed softly, 'it didn't.'

Putting out a hand, he gently pulled the sheet from her fingers, a bright flame of desire in his eyes as they caressed her. 'You realise that if I get into that bed then I'll have to make an honest woman of you, don't you?'

She smiled, her eyes radiant with love and happiness. 'I rather hoped you might,' she admitted.

He leant forward and kissed her long and lingeringly, then reached over to turn out the light.

His voice thick and unsteady, he said, 'Well, on that understanding, my dearest love, you'd better move over.'

THE BERMUDA TRIANGLE

Children growing up in towns on the coast of Florida hear about it in whispered conversations among the grown-ups. Airline pilots flying planeloads of vacationers to Miami tell their passengers half-jokingly not to worry. Worry? About what?

The Florida coast is the western edge of a mysterious area of ocean known as the Bermuda Triangle. Extending to Bermuda in the north and to the mid-Atlantic Sargasso Sea in the east, this triangle of ocean has presented a most intriguing mystery. For it is here in the Bermuda Triangle that countless ships and airplanes are alleged to have vanished into thin air; from some people sailing through or flying above the Triangle there have been reports of the sudden malfunction of navigational equipment, pulsating lights in the sky or beneath the sea, the appearance of phantom ships and planes.

Skeptics insist this is balderdash. Of course ships and planes have disappeared, just as they have elsewhere. The Triangle, they point out, is dangerous only because of the drug smuggling and piracy that is unfortunately common in the Caribbean.

But other explanations for the strange occurrences have been offered: mysterious magnetic waves from deep under the ocean; or still functioning power sources for the lost continent of Atlantis, which somehow pull ships and planes down into an ocean grave. Some even suggest that the Bermuda Triangle is part of a space-time warp that could some day lead to interplanetary travel!

Whatever the truth may be, strange things have been observed in this patch of ocean for hundreds of years. As long as the unexplained is intriguing—and when will it not be—the Bermuda Triangle is sure to fascinate people for hundreds of years to come.

What readers say about Harlequin romance fiction...

"You're #1."

A.H.,* Hattiesburg, Missouri

"Thank you for the many hours of lovely enjoyment you have given me."

M.M., Schaumburg, Illinois

"The books are so good that I have to read them all the way through before being able to go to sleep at night."

N.Q., Newark, California

"Thanks for many happy hours."

M.L., Millville, New Jersey

"Harlequin books are the doorway to pleasure."

E.W., Hawthorne, California

"They are quality books—down-to-earth reading! Don't ever quit!"

G.F., Buffalo, Minnesota

"A pleasant escape from the pressures of this world."

C.T., Hickory, North Carolina

"Keep them coming! They are still the best books."

R.W., Jersey City, New Jersey

*Names available on request

FREE!
Romance Treasury

**A beautifully bound,
value-packed,
three-in-one
volume of romance!**

Complete and mail today the FREE gift certificate and subscription reservation on the following page.

Romance Treasury

An exciting opportunity to collect treasured works of romance! Almost 600 pages of exciting romance reading in each beautifully bound hardcover volume!

You may cancel your subscription whenever you wish! You don't have to buy any minimum number of volumes. Whenever you decide to stop your subscription just drop us a line and we'll cancel all further shipments.

"I'll pay you back when we arrive...."

Michelle's voice was unsteady, but she stood her ground, even when Guy retorted, "The answer's still no. If I agreed to accept pay, you'd expect me to feed you and run around for you as well as sail the boat. No, you'll work, young lady—even if you think you're too good for that kind of thing."

Michelle yelled back at him, "I'm not doing any more of your filthy horrible jobs!"

"All right," he answered, "if you won't work your passage as crew then you'll have to work it the other way. There has to be something you're good at. Maybe it's this...."

And taking hold of her arm, he pulled her firmly toward him, bending his mouth to her lips....

SALLY
WENTWORTH

the sea master

Harlequin Books

TORONTO • LONDON • LOS ANGELES • AMSTERDAM
SYDNEY • HAMBURG • PARIS • STOCKHOLM • ATHENS • TOKYO

Harlequin Presents edition published July 1982
ISBN 0-373-10512-6

Original hardcover edition published in 1982
by Mills & Boon Limited